AF596431

The Imaginary Kingdom Of Children

LE GRASSE Roger-Pierre

Printed by: **Printing under contract with Amazon, Inc.**

Legal deposit: **March 2023**

ISBN: **978-2-493146-09-0**

Price: **US$ 16.00**

LE GRASSE ROGER-PIERRE – 36 RUE DU MAGASIN – 45130 EPIEDS-EN-BEAUCE – FRANCE

DÉDICACE

To all those who have kept their child's soul and who continue to believe in the power of imagination, this book is dedicated to you. May you find in these pages an escape to a world where everything is possible, and dreams come true. Thank you for believing in the magic of writing.

TABLE DES MATIÈRES

DÉDICACE v

TABLE DES MATIÈRES vii

REMERCIEMENTS...ix

1 – BEFORE HISTORY. 1

2 – THE FIGHT. 5

3 – THE IMAGINARY WORLD...............................27

4 – BRYAN'S QUEST..45

5 – ALICE'S SECRET. 63

6 – THE FOREST OF RIDDLES..............................85

7 – THE CRYSTAL LABYRINTH. 111

8 – REVELATION...135

9 – THE BLACK MARKET. 159

10 – THE LAST HOPE...183

11 – RETURN HOME. 207

12 – AFTER. 237

ABOUT THE AUTHOR 257

REMERCIEMENTS

I want to thank my family from the bottom of my heart for their unconditional support throughout the creation of this novel. Your love and support have been my inspiration and has allowed me to pursue my dreams.

A huge thank you also to Stephanie Marie Hylard, for her precious help and advice that was of great help and made this novel even better.

I am also grateful to my friends who have encouraged and supported me throughout this journey. Your support and encouragement have been an important source of motivation.

Finally, I would like to thank all those who supported me in the realization of this book, whether directly or indirectly. Without your help, this project would not have been possible.

Thank you all for your support and love.

1 – BEFORE HISTORY.

Slidewater is a city in the United States of America in the state of Georgia. It has about ten thousand inhabitants and is characterized by its peaceful and warm atmosphere. The city is offered by a green nature and is bordered by a river that runs through the city and gives it its name.

Downtown is typical of small American towns, with streets lined with colonial-style houses, local businesses, and a neighborhood vibe. There is a public park with a playground, benches to sit on and a pond where you can fish. Locals often get to know each other, and neighbors greet each other with friendship.

There is a primary school and a secondary school in the city, both of modest size, where students are known by their first names and receive a quality education. The city is proud of its local football team that brings locals together at home games.

The town also has a small hospital, library, local museum, church, post office, supermarket, pharmacy, and a few local restaurants. There is an open-air cinema that is open during the summer months.

Slidewater is a peaceful and welcoming town that offers a pleasant quality of life to its inhabitants. Local traditions are strong, and locals are proud of their city. Local events, such as city parties, Thanksgiving and Christmas celebrations, are strong times to bring the community together and strengthen social bonds.

Walter is a fourteen-year-old boy who lives in the small town of Slidewater, Georgia in the United States. He is about one meter sixty-five tall and weighs about sixty kilos. Walter has dark brown hair, green eyes, and fair skin. He has a thin face and regular features. He is healthy, but he is quite thin and lacks muscle.

Walter is currently in ninth grade, which is the second year of high school in the United States. He attended Slidewater High School, which was the only secondary school in the city. Walter has always been an average student when it comes to academic performance. It does not have any major difficulty in the subjects, but it does not stand out either. His favorite subjects are history and literature, while mathematics is one of his weakest subjects.

Walter is an introverted and reserved young boy. He doesn't have many friends at school and doesn't participate in extracurricular activities. He spends most of his free time reading or playing video games, which is a source of escape for him. He struggles to open up to others and build deep relationships with people. Walter has a rather distant relationship with his parents, although he respects and appreciates them. He often feels lonely and isolated, which pushes him to look for ways to distract and entertain himself.

Walter's parents are John and Mary. John is a businessman and Mary is a lawyer. They both work in Atlanta, the nearby town of Slidewater, and often have to leave early in the morning and return late at night. They try as much as possible to spend time with their son on weekends and holidays, but their professional activities make them both very busy. John is a tall and elegant man, with brown hair and green eyes. Mary, on the other hand, is smaller than her husband, but has a strong personality. She has short blonde hair and bright blue eyes. Despite their busy schedules, they try to give their son everything he needs to succeed in life. They are proud of his academic success and encourage him to pursue his dreams and passions.

2 – THE FIGHT.

Walter wakes up slowly, trying to get rid of the accumulated fatigue of the previous night. He rubs his eyes and straightens up to get out of bed. He glances at the wall clock and realizes he's late. He hurries out of bed and heads to the bathroom to brush his teeth and take a quick shower. As he washes, he can't help but think about the day ahead.

He is in ninth grade and this year is very important to him because he needs to start thinking in a simplified way about his future and his higher education choices. He feels a little stressed and anxious about having to make such decisions, but he tries to keep a positive mindset.

Walter leaves the bathroom, still drying his hair with a towel. He heads to his room to get dressed. You need a simple outfit: jeans and a sweatshirt and put on your sports shoes. He feels ready for the day ahead.

Walter goes down to the kitchen where his father is preparing breakfast. He smiles when he sees his son and gives him a quick hand to prepare a bowl of cereal and a slice of toast. Mary, Walter's mother, has already left for work, but she always leaves a note to encourage her son and wish him a good day.

Walter sits down at the kitchen table to have breakfast and chat with his father. John asks him how his night was and if he is ready for school. Walter responds briefly, tempted not to let his stress show. John seems to notice his son's-tired expression and asks him if there is anything wrong. Walter shakes his head and replies that everything is fine.

After finishing his breakfast, Walter gets up from the table and heads to the front door. John follows him and gives him a warm hug before wishing him a good day. Walter opens the door and heads to the bus stop, ready for the challenges of the day.

As Walter gets on the bus to the school, he feels a lump in his stomach. He knows he has to take an important exam today and that makes him a little anxious. During the bus ride, he looks out the window and watches the streets of Slidewater pass past him. He tries to focus on the beauty of the streets, houses, trees, and gardens he sees, but his mind keeps coming back to the exam he has to take.

When he arrives at school, Walter joins his usual group of friends with whom he chats and jokes. He tries to get in the mood, but he can't help but think about the exam that awaits him. His friends notice that he is a little quiet and ask if there is anything wrong. Walter explains that he is nervous about taking this important exam.

His friends try to reassure him that he is smart and that he has studied for this exam. They also encourage him by telling him that if he has problems, they are there to help him. This comforts Walter a little, but he remains worried about the exam.

Once they've taken their books from their respective lockers, Walter, and his friends head to their first hour of class. Their conversations are lively, and they joke happily as they walk the halls. However, Walter stays a little behind and listens more than he speaks. He always feels anxious and concerned.

Walter's friends immediately notice that he is not in his usual state. They greet him enthusiastically, but Walter does not answer as usual, he is content with their smile faintly in response. His friends are aware that there is something wrong, so they ask him if there is a problem. Walter hesitates for a moment before explaining to them that he has an important exam today and that he is nervous about it. His friends are understanding and give him encouragement, saying that if he has worked hard, he will succeed.

However, Walter is too absorbed in his own thoughts to really listen to what his friends have to say. He looks around distractedly, watching the other students prepare for the day. He feels like everyone is talking and laughing, but he can't help but feel isolated and alone. He feels like no one can understand the pressure he feels to succeed.

Walter has tried to convince himself that everything will be fine, but he is overwhelmed by anxiety and doubts. He feels that if he does not pass this exam, it could jeopardize his future. His friends keep telling him he's going to be fine, but he can't calm down. He feels that the hours before the exam pass slowly and that every minute is torture.

Finally, it's exam time, and Walter has to focus on the task at hand. He walks into his classroom with a mixture of fear and determination. His friends greet him with smiles of encouragement, but he is too focused on the exam to answer them.

Walter enters the exam room, trying to calm down before taking his seat. He looks around the room, assessing the students who are silent, wondering how many of them are as nervous as he is. Then, the teacher begins to distribute the exam papers, and everyone plunges into silence.

After a few hours, the results of the examination arrive. Walter feels relieved to have passed it and can't wait to see how he managed. However, when he receives his grade, he realizes that he has obtained an average grade. Walter felt a little discouraged, but he remembers that this exam was particularly difficult, and he worked very hard to prepare for it. He realizes that he should be proud of his performance and that he can use this experience to improve in the future.

As he walks to his locker to store his belongings, Stephan, a student in his class, approaches him and mocks his grade.

Stephan: Ha! Look who's there, the failure of the class! So how did you fare in the exam, Walter?

Walter: *(frowning)* You don't need to make fun of me, Stephan. My rating does not define who I am as a person.

Stephan: *(laughing)* Oh, but of course it is! You're just a loser who can't achieve anything.

Walter: *(clenched fists)* Stop saying that! I worked during this exam, and even though I got an average grade, I'm proud of myself because I did my best.

Stephan: *(continuing to laugh)* You're pathetic. You will never achieve anything in life.

Walter: *(breathing deeply)* You don't know anything about me, Stephan. I am able to achieve anything I want if I work hard enough. Instead of making fun of me, you'd better focus on your own business.

Stephan: *(continuing to laugh)* You are the biggest moron in the state of Georgia my poor.

Walter: *(getting angrier)* You don't know anything about me, Stephan. You don't know what I'm capable of doing. You don't have the right to judge me like that!

Stephan: *(scoffing)* Oh, listen to him! He tries to defend himself, but all he can do is stammer.

Walter: *(beside himself)* You're going to stop making fun of me right now! *(He pushes Stephan, who falls to the ground.)*

Stephan: *(furious)* How dare you touch me, you loser? *(He gets up and pushes Walter back.)*

The situation quickly escalates, and a fight breaks out between Walter and Stephan. The other students in the class take the opportunity to gather around the two boys and watch the show.

Walter: *(taking a punch)* Ouch! *(He retaliates by kicking Stephan.)*

Stephan: *(avoiding the blow and rushing at Walter)* I'll show you who's the boss here! *(He starts punching Walter)*

The fight between Walter and Stephan quickly escalated. The two boys grabbed each other and started punching and kicking each other. Walter had raged in his stomach, while Stephan continued to provoke and belittle him. The other students who crowded in the hallway tried to separate them, but to no avail.

Suddenly, Stephan punched Walter violently and made him waver. Walter hit the water fountain behind him and lost his balance.

His head hit the edge of the fountain before he collapsed to the ground.

The screams and screams provided the attention of the other students who rushed to the scene of the incident. Some stood still, shocked by the scene, while others immediately ran for help. The math teacher patrolling the hallways that day was one of the first to arrive at the scene of the incident. He called for help and ordered the other students to calm down and back away to make room for health workers.

Meanwhile, Walter was lying on the ground, motionless and unconscious. His face was pale, and his breathing was weak. The students who had stayed close to him tried to resuscitate him by slapping him on the cheeks and trying to get him back to him. But their efforts came to nothing. Everyone was shocked and feared for Walter.

Fortunately, help arrived quickly on the scene, accompanied by an ambulance and a competent medical team. They immediately took care of Walter and transported him to Slidewater Hospital for urgent surgery. The other students, still in shock, followed the emergency services with their eyes, worried about the condition of their classmate.

This incident left everyone in shock and reminded all students of the serious consequences of acts of violence. News of the incident quickly spread throughout the school, causing a great shock among students and teachers. Walter's parents were informed of the incident and went to the hospital to be by his side. Teachers and school authorities held meetings to discuss the importance of mutual respect and the need to behave responsibly and respect others.

Meanwhile, Walter remained in a deep sleep. The doctors did everything they could to wake him up, but he was still in a coma.

Walter was immediately admitted to intensive care. Doctors performed several tests to determine the extent of the damage from Walter's fall, but it was too early to make an accurate diagnosis. Walter's parents were devastated and terrified of losing their only son. They wondered if it was their fault. They had not been more present for him, and they had not noticed the warning signs of the harassment their son was experiencing.

The doctor explained to them that Walter was in a coma and would be closely monitored by the caregivers. The doctor specialized in neurology emergency, the doctor. Williams entered the hospital waiting room. Mary and John, young Walter's parents, rose from their seats, anxious to know the state of their son Walter's health.

Dr. Williams: Good morning, Mr. Jones. I am Dr. Williams, the neurologist-emergency physician responsible for Walter. I am sorry to inform you that your son's condition is very concerning. He is in a deep coma following a traumatic brain injury caused by a fight.

Mary: Oh, my God, does that mean Walter isn't going to wake up?

"We can't predict the future, but it's important for you to know that his brain has suffered significant damage. We have done surgery to reduce intracranial pressure, but there is still a lot of work to be done." Answers the emergency neurologist.

"What should we do now, doctor?" Father Walter's asked.

Dr. Williams: We're going to keep Walter under close surveillance and keep him sedated to reduce his brain activity and allow his brain to heal. We will also perform regular tests to monitor his brain activity and make sure there are no further complications.

Mary: What if he doesn't wake up? What happens next?

Dr. Williams: If Walter doesn't wake up, he could be in a vegetative state or a state of minimal consciousness. We will continue to provide supportive care to ensure their comfort and quality of life, but it's important for you to know that this could be a long journey for you and your family.

John: We'll do whatever Walter needs. We are ready to support it, no matter what happens.

Mary: He's our son, we love him, and we want him to get better.

Dr. Williams: I understand and I'm here to help you through this difficult time. We will do everything we can to help Walter recover, but I want you to be prepared for all possibilities.

Walter's parents nodded, tears in their eyes, emotions overwhelming them. They knew their son needed their support and that they were willing to do whatever it took for him. Dr. Williams assured them that he would do everything in his power to help Walter heal.

Walter's parents spent the first few hours in the hospital at his bedside, praying that their son would wake up soon. They asked themselves what they could do to help their son, how could they get him out of this situation? Emotions were running high, and Walter's father finally broke the silence.

"Do you think it's our fault?" he asked his wife.

"Of our fault?" she repeated, staring lost in the void. "How could it be our fault?"

"Maybe we should have noticed something, paid more attention to our son," he said, his face grave.

"We did our best," Walter's mother replied. "We've always supported it, but we couldn't foresee that. It was Stephan and the others who did that, not us."

Walter's parents were deeply sad. They couldn't believe their son was in a coma. Tears streamed down their faces as they comforted each other. They wondered how they were going to deal with this situation and how they were going to find the strength to continue.

As the hours passed, they exchanged stories and memories of their son. They talked about his personality, his tastes, his dreams, and everything that made him unique. They recalled happy moments spent together, such as family vacations, trips to the park, birthdays, Christmases, and movie nights.

Speaking of their son, they understood that it was now more than ever time to stay united and support Walter. They promised to do everything in their power to help their son through this difficult ordeal. They decided to put aside their differences and work together to find a solution.

Despite their pain, they tried to stay positive and hopeful. They prayed for their son to recover quickly and asked their friends and family to do the same.

Eventually, Walter's parents realized that their love for their son was stronger than anything. They were determined to stay strong and be there for their son no matter what happened.

Walter's parents were eventually allowed to see their son, who was still in a coma. Upon entering the hospital room, they were shocked to see Walter hooked up to various devices and tubes, and to see his face so pale and motionless. They held back their tears and took their seats next to her bed.

Doctors explained that Walter had suffered a severe concussion and was in critical condition. They said they could not guarantee his recovery and that they had to be prepared for any eventuality in the face of the damage their son might have afterwards.

Walter's parents spent days in the hospital, waiting for their son to wake up. Meanwhile, they prayed and hoped that their son would recover soon. They also received support from friends and family, who continued to provide them with food and encouragement.

During those difficult days, Walter's parents realized that life was fragile and that every moment was precious. They began to focus on the happy times they had spent together with their son and began to envision a future where he would fully recover. They also began looking for ways to support Walter when he was discharged from the hospital.

Days turned into weeks and weeks turned into months, but Walter still showed no signs of waking up. The parents began to wonder if their son would ever wake up and began to consider the worst situation.

They began seeking information about palliative care options, fearing that their son would suffer unnecessarily. However, they never gave up hope that Walter would wake up one day.

Parents also began to notice that many students at Walter's high school made visits to the hospital to check on their friend. They were touched by the solidarity of the community and were re-grateful for their support. They spent time talking to Walter's friends, sharing memories of their son, and exchanging stories about their friendship with him.

Meanwhile, Walter's parents also made difficult decisions, including whether to continue their son's medical care. They decided to continue the intensified care, even if it meant an ever-increasing hospital bill. They knew that their son was much loved and wanted to give Walter every chance of survival.

Despite the uncertainty and pain they felt, Walter's parents continued to be united and supportive of their son. They remained hopeful and prayed that their son would one day recover.

Meanwhile, professors in turn regularly connected to the hospital to check on him. Some of them were professors who taught Walter, while others knew him simply by sight. They were all affected by Walter's accident and wanted to show their support for his family.

When they arrived at the hospital, Walter's parents greeted them warmly. Students and teachers often asked how Walter was doing and worried about his condition. The parents honestly explained the situation, telling them that their son still showed no signs of waking up.

The students and teachers at the high school were sad to hear this, but they remained positive and hoped Walter would recover soon. They offered their help and support to Walter's family, telling them they were there for them in these difficult times.

Walter's parents were touched by their kindness and support. It gave them hope and allowed them to see that their son had touched the lives of many people.

Meanwhile, the parents began to think about how they could help their son when he was discharged from the hospital. They began to look for alternative therapies and learn about rehabilitation programs. They knew that the road to Walter's recovery would be long and difficult, but they were willing to do everything they could to support their son.

Walter's parents contacted specialists in the field of rehabilitation and scheduled a series of therapy sessions for Walter as soon as he came out of his coma. They also began investigating more intensive rehabilitation programs that might be needed for Walter in the event that he didn't wake up quickly.

Meanwhile, Walter's friends from high school continued to come to the hospital to check on him. They were shocked to see their friend in such a state and were very concerned about his health. Walter's parents were touched by the support of these young men and found comfort in the fact that their son had friends who cared so much about him.

Parents have also started talking to support groups for families with loved ones in a coma, seeking advice on how best to support their son and cope with the difficult situation in which they stand out.

They realized that Walter's road to recovery would be long and difficult, but they were determined to do everything they could to help their son overcome it. They continued to pray for his recovery and hope that their son would wake up soon.

3 – THE IMAGINARY WORLD.

When Walter woke up, he was surprised to find himself in a totally different world. He looked around, amazed. The buildings were identical to those he had known in the real world, but there was something strange about the way everything worked. The children he saw running in the streets were busy doing tasks that adults would normally do some were building houses, others were working in gardens or on farms, while still others were selling goods in local markets.

Everything seemed well organized, and the children worked together with great efficiency. This presented Walter with the impression that this world was real, but in a way different from anything he had known before. He notices that the children all seemed happy and carefree, as if they had no worries in the world.

As Walter explored this world further, he began to notice details that made him even stranger. The road signs were all written in strange and unknown languages, but he could understand them without any problem. The animals he saw were different from the ones he knew, but he could name them effortlessly. Everything seems almost normal, but with subtle and strange differences.

Walter wondered what could have happened to make the children the only ones working and running this world. He was desperately looking for a way to understand what was going on, but he didn't understand and couldn't find an answer. He was intrigued by this imaginary world and wanted to know more, but he knew that for now, he just had to keep exploring this mysterious new world.

Walter couldn't figure out how this was possible, but all the adults had mysteriously disappeared from this imaginary world. The children seemed to be the only ones running this strange world. Despite the absence of adults, this world was very organized, as if children knew exactly what to do. The older ones took care of the younger ones, took care of food and water, and managed the affairs of the community.

Walter noticed that this imaginary world looked a lot like the real world, but with subtle differences. For example, cars were smaller and more colorful, buildings were made from eco-friendly materials and there was no pollution. The children seemed to have taken control and created their own utopian society. However, despite all the wonderful things he saw, Walter was worried that he didn't know how he got into this fantasy world, and if he could ever get out of it.

Walter continued to explore the imaginary world he woke up in and noticed that the children seemed to perform the work of the adults, but in a playful and creative way. They incorporated colorful houses that were made from materials such as wood and bamboo, and transformed the streets into vast play areas, complete with slides, swings and sports fields. They seemed to have a balanced social organization, with respected leaders among older children and an equitable distribution of resources and tasks.

Walter also observed that children seemed to have developed advanced technology for their age, such as advanced communication devices. But despite all this progress, there was something mysterious about the imaginary world. Walter couldn't understand how it was all created or how he ended up in this strange world.

However, he continued to explore, eager to find answers to his questions. He began to notice abnormalities in the children's behavior, as if they had something to hide or were nervous around him. Walter began to wonder if it was possible that this fantasy world was created for a specific reason and was placed in it for a mission. He needed answers, but he didn't know who to ask or how to find them.

The children's houses were like mini palaces, each building unique and tastefully decorated. Some had colored glass walls that sparkled under the sun's rays, while others were covered with climbing plants. Fruit trees grew in the gardens, and children picked them to prepare delicious meals. Each house had a flag or banner flying that showcased its family and values. Astonishing towers rose into the sky, their tops disappearing into the clouds. There were slides and swings attached to the tallest buildings, and suspension bridges over the streets. The children seemed to be experts in construction and design, tuned amazing structures with eco-friendly materials.

The children watching Walter seemed to be intrigued by his presence, as if he were a stranger in their own world. They looked at him with astonished and curious eyes, but never approached him. Walter wondered why he was the object of their attention, but he also felt amazed by them and their way of life. He observed their behavior and interaction, and he was amazed by their ability to work together to maintain their utopian society. They had strict but fair rules to make sure everyone was taken care of, and even the youngest children were involved in community tasks. Walter was beginning to realize that he had a lot to learn from these children, despite his age.

The sky was bright blue and there were white clouds floating in the air. Walter saw crystal clear rivers and magnificent waterfalls, with rainbows that seemed to stretch to infinity. There were animals everywhere, rabbits, deer, birds, and even horses galloping through the flower fields.

Walter felt as if he had entered another world, a world that existed only in his mind. Everything seemed so real, so beautiful, so magical. He continued to explore this imaginary world, fascinated by everything he saw.

Walter felt more and more involved in the world of children, but he still had unanswered questions about how he got into this imaginary world. He was desperately looking for an answer.

Walter walked timidly towards the central square of the city, where Alice and Elliot were standing. As he approached, he could see that Alice was a young girl about fifteen years old, with long curly brown hair falling over her shoulders. She had sparked green eyes and a warm smile stretching across her face when she saw Walter. She was dressed in a light cloth dress that fluttered slightly in the wind, adorned with a golden star-shaped badge on her chest.

Elliot, meanwhile, was a younger boy than Alice, with tousled blonde hair and a slightly upturned nose. He had bright blue eyes and a mischievous smile that appeared on his face when he saw Walter approaching. He was wearing a light-colored shirt with matching pants and brown leather shoes.

Alice stood up from her chair smiling at Walter, while Elliot jumped from the railing, he was sitting on to join them. Walter immediately felt at ease with the two children, who explained to him the principles of their company and commented that they had managed to keep it in place. Alice explained in detail how she was elected to lead the city and how she worked hard to ensure that everyone had a place in their utopian world. Elliot recounted how he helped Alice build the city and how he learned to grow their own food.

Walter was impressed by their determination and commitment to their company. He realized that despite their young age, Alice and Elliot had wisdom and insight far beyond their years. They were also very open-minded and welcoming to him, a stranger who had just arrived in their fantasy world.

Alice and Elliot greet Walter with warm smiles and ask him how he landed in their world. Walter briefly explained his story to them, but they seemed more signified by how he could contribute to their community. Alice, the town's leader, began to ask him questions about his skills and experience, while Elliot listened intently.

Walter was impressed by the way Alice spoke confidently and made decisions with the needs of everyone in the community in mind. She seems to have a great ability to listen to others and solve problems creatively. Elliot, meanwhile, seemed to be a loyal and supposed friend of Alice, ready to support her in all her decisions.

During the dialogue, Alice explained the rules of their society and how they managed to maintain their utopia by respecting these rules. She stressed the importance of cooperation and equity in maintaining peace and prosperity. Elliot, for his part, added some anecdotes about how the community had solved difficult problems by working together.

Walter was impressed by their vision and determination, but he couldn't help but wonder if he had a place in this ideal world. Alice seemed to have noticed his hesitation and explained that they were always looking for people with different skills and perspectives to continue improving their community. She encouraged him to stay a little longer to learn more about their way of life and think about how he could contribute.

Elliot, for his part, proposes to show Walter the most interesting places in the city and introduce him to the inhabitants. Together, they explore their utopian world, discussing and learning from each other. Walter began to understand that even though he had different knowledge and skills than the people of this world, he could contribute to their community by bringing a new perspective and working with them to maintain their ideal society.

Walter addresses Alice and Elliot by asking them if they knew how he came into their world. Alice shook her head in response, saying she didn't know how he landed here. Elliot added that he had heard that from time to time, strangers came into their world without explanation and were welcomed into their community.

Alice turned to Walter and explained that their city was not unique. She explained that there was a capital of about twenty leagues from their city and that it was run by a man named Bryan. She added that Bryan is responsible for many cities and communities around the world.

Walter was curious to know how Bryan had been appointed to this position of power. Alice explained that Bryan was chosen from among the leaders of various communities to help resolve conflicts and keep the peace. Over time, his reputation had grown, and he was eventually appointed head of all communities.

Elliot added that while they didn't respond to Walter's arrival, they were happy to welcome him into their community and help him find his place here. Alice added that she was sure Bryan would be interested in bringing a new stranger into their world and that she would be happy to take him to the capital to meet Bryan if he wished.

Walter was intrigued by this offer and agreed. He wondered what the future held for him in this strange but fascinating world. The children seemed to have some kind of innate wisdom about how their world worked. Walter began to realize that the world of adults was very different from that of children. He recalled how adults were often preoccupied with material things and power issues, while children seemed to be more concerned with relationships and the well-being of the community.

Walter felt a little relieved to know that he was not the only stranger in this world. He felt that children were more tolerant and welcoming than the adults he had met in his home world. He wondered how the children of this community had learned to live in this strange world and what they had had to face to get there.

Alice noticed the thinking expression on Walter's face and asked what was bothering him. Walter explained that he was fascinated by how children seemed so comfortable in this world, despite the fact that they had arrived here without explanation. He also expressed his amazement at the wisdom and maturity of the children in this community.

Elliot smiled and explained that children in their community must learn to work together to survive in this world. They had learned to stand together and support each other, despite their differences. He also stressed that the community had core values, such as respect, tolerance, and peace, which were instilled from an early age.

Alice added that the community has also set up an education system for children to learn to understand and navigate their world. She explained that each child had a mentor who guided them and helped them find their place in the community.

Walter was impressed by how the community had cared for his children and their well-being. He realized that this could be a model for the adult world in his home world. He expressed his admiration for their approach and philosophy, and a promise to do his best to integrate into their community.

Alice smiled and said she was glad Walter decided to stay with them. Walter was very touched by the warm welcome and approach of the community towards the children. He began to feel at home in this strange, but fascinating world. He was also grateful for the mentorship the children received and wondered if he could also find a mentor to help him adjust to their lifestyle.

Elliot offered to introduce him to his own mentor, a young man named Michael, who had lived in their community for many years and had a deep knowledge of their world. Walter gratefully agreed and was introduced to Michael the next morning.

Michael is a seventeen-year-old boy with an impressive physique. It measures about one meter eighty in height and a slender, but muscular silhouette. He has broad shoulders and a well-developed torso that demonstrates his commitment to physical exercise. His torso and legs are proportioned and muscular, which gives his body an athletic appearance.

His face is angular and symmetrical, with well-defined features. He has thick, dark eyebrows that frame his deep blue eyes. His eyes are large and expressive, and they often exhibit a curious and adventurous personality. It has a straight and thin nose, and a square jaw that gives it a sure and confident expression.

Her dark brown hair is cut short and well groomed, and it frames her face flatteringly. Her skin is tanned, testifying to her passion for outdoor activities such as camping, hiking, and biking. His hands are large and agile, testifying to his ability to use tools and equipment with skill.

Overall, Michael is a young man with an impressive and athletic physique, well-defined features, and expressive eyes. Her appearance is both attractive and intimidating, a testament to her determination and strength of character.

Michael often finds himself facing prejudice from others because of his appearance, but he has learned to ignore and focus on what really matters to him. Despite this, he cares a lot about his appearance and takes care of his body by exercising regularly and eating healthy.

Michael was a gentle and wise man who greeted Walter with a big smile. They began discussing each other's lives and Michael commented on him who had landed in this world and how he had learned to understand and live in it. He also shared tips on how Walter could adapt to their lifestyle and be part of their community.

Walter was fascinated by Michael's stories and was amazed at the wisdom he had gained from living in this world. He was grateful for the guidance he received and began to feel more comfortable in this new life.

As the days went by, Walter got to know the other members of the community and understand their way of life. He also began contributing to the community by using his skills and knowledge to help with daily tasks. He was happy to have found a new family and a new home in this strange world.

Michael quickly realized that Walter needed help integrating into their community and was happy to offer his support. He organized a guided tour of their village and introduced Walter to all members of their community.

Michael was highly respected in their village, not only for his impressive appearance, but also for his friendly and helpful character. He was always willing to help others and do whatever he could to improve life in their community.

Walter was amazed by the natural beauty of their village, with its vast green fields and rolling hills. He was touched by the kindness of each member of the community, who welcomed him with open arms and helped him feel at home.

Over time, Walter began to adapt to their way of life and participate in the daily activities of their village. He helped cultivate fields, repair houses, and take care of animals. He also learned how to cook local dishes and play traditional musical instruments.

Michael was proud to see how Walter had adapted to their lifestyle and was appreciated for his contribution to their community. He saw in him a courageous and hard-working young man with great potential to succeed in their world.

Ultimately, Michael and Walter became good friends, sharing stories and experiences while working together to improve their lives in their community. They learned from each other and created lasting privileges that strengthened their community and allowed them to thrive.

One day, Michael, Walter, Alice, and Elliot decided to throw a party in their community to celebrate their village's new crops and successes. They invited all members of their community as well as neighboring villages to join them.

Alice was an energetic and creative young woman, known for her artistic talents and enterprising spirit. She helped decorate the village square with garlands and colorful balloons, providing a festive atmosphere for all guests.

Elliot was a wise young man, respected in their community for his knowledge and wisdom. He organized a blessing ceremony for the new crops and shared stories from their community's history to remind all guests of the importance of their traditions and heritage.

The party was a great success, with delicious food, lively music, and traditional dances. Members of their community grew closer to their neighbors and shared stories and traditions with them.

Alice had always been very good at throwing parties, but this time she decided to do something really special for their community and surrounding towns. She had worked for weeks to prepare for this party, inviting all the neighbors to come and protest together.

On the day of the festival, people of all ages were present, playing music, dancing, and enjoying delicious food prepared by Alice and other members of the community. Everyone was happy and relaxed, enjoying this festive day.

The party organized by Alice had provided people from all the surrounding towns, granted a joyful and festive atmosphere throughout the village. Everyone mingled, sharing food and drinks, dancing and singing together.

However, there was a very special guest who was present at the party in an incognito manner, Bryan, the prominent member of the Grand Council who was never seen in public. No one knew that it was him, not even Alice who had organized the party, because he had chosen to dress up in a costume that hid him well.

Bryan had heard about the organization of Alice's party and decided to come incognito to see with his own eyes how the people of the village and surrounding towns lived. He was curious to see how they behaved towards each other and how they had fun.

During the evening, Bryan mingled with the crowd, talking with people, and sharing stories with them. No one suspected that he was actually Bryan, as he had done a great job of dressing up and blending into the crowd.

People were amazed by the enthusiasm of this stranger, who behaved like one of their own. He was comfortable with everyone.

Bryan had had an enjoyable evening, enjoyed the party, but also learned about the people and their way of life. By the end of the night, he had quietly left the party, everyone wondering who this mysterious guest was who had conveyed such a cheerful and friendly vibe to Alice's party.

4 – BRYAN'S QUEST.

Walter had listened attentively to Alice and Elliot tell him about the Great Council that ruled the world of children, led by a certain person named Bryan. Since that conversation, he had been plagued by questions. Who was this, Bryan? Where did it come from? How did he get into this world of children? And above all, was this world real or just imaginary?

All these questions were spinning in Walter's head, pushing him to look for answers. He spent long hours observing the children around him, trying to see if there was something different about them, something that made them different from the children he had known before.

He also wondered why he had been transported to this world. Was this just a coincidence, or was there a deeper reason behind it? And if so, what was that reason?

Walter struggled to concentrate on daily tasks, haunted by these unanswered questions. He spends long hours thinking, trying to understand the mysteries of this strange world.

Even so, Walter knew he had to find answers to these questions. He was determined to find out the truth about Bryan and the Great Council, and about the children's world he had been plunged into. He was willing to do anything to find the answers to his questions and discover the truth hidden behind this strange and fascinating world.

Walter was lost in thought, trying to figure out how he could have arrived in this world ruled by a mysterious leader named Bryan. He felt disconnected from reality, wondering if it was all just a dream or if he was really in a parallel world.

He decided to look for answers, to find out who Bryan was and how he could get in touch with him. He asked Alice and Elliot questions, tried to gather information about the Great Council and about Bryan himself.

Walter sat with Alice and Elliot, listening intently to their stories about Bryan, the mysterious ruler of the children's world. They shared all the information they had heard about him but admitted that they had never met the chief themselves.

Alice began to explain, "All we know about Bryan is that he is the head of the Great Council, and he rules our world. No one has ever seen his face, and it is said that it is very secretive."

Elliot added, “Some people say he has the power to control time and can make magical items appear, but we can’t confirm those rumors.”

Walter was puzzled and asked, “But how did I get here, then? And how can I get out of this world if no one knows who rules this world?”

Alice replied, “That’s a question we don’t have an answer to. All we know is that you are here, and that if you want to find a way to leave. It’s clear that it’s Bryan you need to see because he plays a crucial role in this world, and we need to find a way to get you to meet him to find out more.”

Over time, Walter discovered that Bryan was considered a fair leader and loved by all. He had succeeded in uniting all the factions of this world of children and in establishing a lasting peace. He was also a conservationist and had policies in place to protect the environment.

Walter began to be fascinated by Bryan and wanted to know more about him. He decides to go in search of this mysterious leader, determined to meet him in person and discover the truth about this strange and fascinating world.

After talking with Alice and Elliot, Walter made the decision to find Bryan so he could ask him the questions Bryan had in his mind. Walter was determined to find Bryan, this mysterious child. After gathering information about the Temple of Wisdom, he learned that Bryan had been seen in the City of Glass, the capital of the Children's World. This city was known for its incredible beauty, built entirely of glass, and illuminated with a thousand colors at nightfall.

Walter had carefully prepared his trip. He had managed to get a card and make provisions for a few days. Knowing that he had to go to a region and a city that was unknown to him. Walter continued his investigation by questioning the people he met on his way. He first met a young child who was selling fruit on the side of the road. She told him that the Temple of Wisdom was a very special place for the people of the region, and that it was often pointed out by children in search of wisdom and knowledge. She also advised him to be careful on the road to the temple, as it was narrow and dangerous.

Walter continued on his way and met a young boy who was herding a flock of sheep. He asked him if he had seen a child named Bryan, and the boy told him that he had seen a child who matched Bryan's description, who had taken the road to the Temple of Wisdom a few days ago. He also advised her to watch out for the dangers that awaited her on the road. The road was winding, lined with spectacular scenery and large, majestic hills. The landscape changed rapidly, from vast green fields to lush forests, and finally to the city of Glass, which stood majestically before him.

The City of Glass was an architectural marvel, with glass buildings sparkling in all directions. Walter finally arrives at the gate of the city of Glass, the capital of the Children's World. The townspeople were all children, but they seemed well organized and had their own system of governance. Walter was immediately struck by the beauty of the city, with its glass buildings and streets lined with colorful flowers.

He searched again for information about Bryan, and eventually met a group of children playing in a fountain. He asked them if they had seen a child named Bryan, and they replied that they did not know him. But one of the children told him that he had heard of a child who had ascended to the Temple of Wisdom a few days before.

He began his investigation to find Bryan. He toured the city, talked to locals, and visited tourist spots. Despite his efforts, he couldn't find Bryan. He was discouraged, but he knew he couldn't give up. He decided to continue his search, hoping to find clues that would eventually lead him to Bryan.

Walter then asked them if they knew how to get to the Temple of Wisdom, and they showed him the way to go. Before leaving, Walter asked them if they knew where he could find food and shelter for the night. The children directed him to a hotel in the center of the city.

Walter walked into the hotel and asked the owner if he could get a meal and room for the night. The young child, about fifteen years old, pointed him to a table where he could sit, and served him a dish of hot soup and fresh bread. As he ate, he overheard lively conversations between hotel guests, all children talking about their daily lives and adventures.

Suddenly, an older child approached him and asked if he was looking for someone. Walter replied that he was looking for a child named Bryan, who had been seen at the Temple of Wisdom. The child told him that he had seen Bryan there and pointed out another route he needed to take to get to the temple faster. Walter thanked him and finished his meal before heading to his room to rest for the night.

Walter began to investigate where he might be. This city was considered beautiful and one of a kind. It was called "City of Glass" because of its transparent and luminous glass buildings that seemed to shine like diamonds under the sun.

The streets of the Glass City were wide and spacious, lined with trees and lush gardens. The buildings were all made of colored glass, offering beautiful views of the city from inside and out. The children were dressed in colorful and cheerful outfits, which added even more color to this already dazzling city.

Walter continued his research and eventually discovered that the Temple of Wisdom was located on top of a hill. This hill was located outside the City of Glass but was still considered an important place for the inhabitants. The hill offered stunning views of the Glass City and the surrounding area, with green fields and fruit trees as far as the eye can see.

Walter took the steep and dangerous road to the top of the hill, hoping to find Bryan at the Temple of Wisdom. The road was winding and narrow, lined with dizzying precipices. However,

Walter was determined to find Bryan and he continued his climb with courage and determination.

He then began to investigate the scene and interview the people he met. He discovered that Bryan had indeed been seen in the temple a few days before. Walter continued his investigation at the scene, questioning those present at the temple and attempting to trace Bryan's movements. He finally managed to find clues that led him to believe that Bryan had left the temple and was heading to another destination.

Thus, Walter continued his research using the information he had gathered at the Temple of Wisdom to pursue Bryan's track. He was able to advance in his investigation and get closer and closer to this famous and enigmatic Bryan.

Walter followed the clues he had collected and ended up arriving in a small town outside the City of Glass. He went to a small restaurant to eat and started asking people about Bryan's presence in the area. He eventually met a girl named Alexia who told him that she had seen a young boy matching Bryan's description pass through the city a few days before.

Walter was very happy to hear this news and continued to speak with Alexia to get more information. She told him that she had heard the boy say he was heading to a place called "the hill of four winds.", but she didn't know exactly where. Walter thanked Alexia for her information and decided to go immediately in search of Bryan.

Walter left the restaurant warmly thanking Alexia for her help. He immediately began to search for information about the Hill of the Four Winds, but he realized that it was very little known in the area. Despite this, he persisted and finally managed to find someone who had heard of this place.

After gathering information on the hill, Walter prepared his travel gear and started walking in the direction indicated by Alexia. He walked for hours in the surrounding countryside, through fields and forests, following a rough map he had drawn. He was determined to find Bryan and learn more about the mysterious world of children.

After a long walk, Walter finally arrived at the foot of a hill that rises majestically in front of him. He looked around and saw that the hill was wrapped in golden wheat fields that swayed gently in the wind. He also noticed that the top of the hill was covered with bushy trees and thorny bushes. He then remembered what Alexia had told him: the Hill of the Four Winds was a sacred place for the ancient inhabitants of the region.

Walter began to climb the hill, following a steep path that meandered through trees and bushes. He had to show a lot of courage to face the obstacles that stood in his way, but he was determined to reach the top and find Bryan.

After climbing for a while, Walter finally got to the top of the hill. He looked around and saw an amazing panoramic view. There was a light breeze blowing, and he could feel the fresh, pure air on his face. He noticed that the view was clear in all directions, and he understood why this place was so important to the people of the area.

The hill was called "the Hill of the Four Winds" because it was said that the four winds blew here at the same time. Walter felt a strong mystical energy in this place, and he thought that this place was a place of power. He knew that if he wanted to find Bryan, he had to look for signs that indicated where he had gone.

Walter began searching for clues on the top of the hill, scanning the ground and surroundings for any trace of Bryan. After a few minutes of searching, he finally found a footprint in the dust. He followed in the footsteps for a while, using all his tracking skills to keep track of Bryan.

He roamed the hill of the four winds for hours, managing to follow the clues in Bryan's footsteps. Finally, he came across a small wooden cabin among the trees, and he heard voices inside.

Walter was slowly approaching the wooden hut when suddenly, a group of children appeared in front of him, interposing their bodies between him and the hut. Walter immediately became suspicious, wondering why these children were there and whether they were there to protect him or to hold him back. As he took a closer look at the children, he realized he recognized one. It was the same boy who had shown him a route to get to the Temple of Wisdom at the hotel. Walter then remembered the circumstances in which the boy had been so helpful and wondered if his help was not a plan to keep him away from Bryan.

The children then began to ask him questions about his identity and why he was there. Walter responded calmly by explaining that he was looking for Bryan and that he had information that could help find him. The children then exchanged glances with each other, hesitating about the way forward. Finally, a little boy walked up to Walter and said, "I'm Billy, one of Striker's friends. If you want to find Bryan, you have to come with us."

Walter followed the children through the trees to a small wooden hut. Inside, he saw five people sitting around a table talking. It was small, but comfortable, with a fireplace and a cot. All around, there were toys, books and board games scattered around, giving the impression that the hut was being used by children. It was a peaceful and quiet place, away from the hustle and bustle of the city. He immediately recognized one of the boys as the one who had helped him find the Temple of Wisdom, and he remembered that his name was Jake.

Jake got up from the table and approached Walter smiling. "I knew you were going to come this far! What are you looking for and what do you want to know?" He told her. Walter quickly explained that he was looking for Bryan and had information to help him find him. Jake nodded and replied, "I see. Unfortunately, we are in the middle of an important meeting right now. If you want, you can wait with us, and we can discuss all this later."

Walter nodded and sat down next to Jake. The other members of the meeting also seemed to be awaited by Walter's presence and warmly welcomed him. There were two girls, one with curly blonde hair and the other with black hair tied in a ponytail, as well as two other boys in addition to Jake and Billy. All seemed to be between ten and sixteen years old.

Walter watches the meeting silently for a moment. The children were discussing something important, but he couldn't understand what it was. He wondered if these children were Bryan's close guard and if their meeting had anything to do with him. But before he could ask questions, one of the children stood up to announce that the meeting was over, and everyone had to leave.

Walter was about to ask Jake what it was, but he realized that the kids were leaving quickly, and it was time for him to leave too. Jake motioned for her to follow him, and the two of them walked out of the cabin and headed for an unknown destination. Walter was curious about what was going on and wondered if the kids would lead him to Bryan.

Walter and Jake had walked for hours through cities of various architectures. The first town they passed through was a small stone town, with narrow streets and white stone buildings that all looked the same. The inhabitants seemed to be artisans and traders, as the streets were filled with shops of all kinds. The second city was larger, with taller and more modern buildings, built of glass and steel. Skyscrapers rose into the sky, shading the streets crowded with cars and people in a hurry.

The third city they passed through was very different from the previous two. It was a coastal town with a large golden sandy beach and colonial-style buildings that seemed reminiscent of a bygone era. Palm trees and exotic flowers lined the streets, and the sound of waves crashing on the shore was soothing.

After passing through the coastal town, Walter and Jake entered a dense forest, following a narrow path that leads them to a small village. It was a picturesque place, with wooden and stone cottages, surrounded by flower gardens. The inhabitants seemed to live in harmony with nature, with green fields and freely roaming animals.

After several hours of walking, Walter and Jake finally arrived at their destination. However, something seemed familiar to Walter in this city. The buildings and streets seemed to remind him of something. Then he realized that this was the city from which he had left a few days earlier. It was back to square one. Jake had driven Walter to the town where it all began. Walter was puzzled and wondered what the meaning of all this was.

While Walter was still acclimatizing to the strangeness of Children's City, Jake told him they had arrived. They were in front of the house of Alice, the leader of the children. Jake said to Alice, "We're bringing you, our friend. The Grand Council will come soon to discuss this with you and Elliot."

5 – ALICE'S SECRET.

Walter experiences a strange scene in a business in the city. A child who wanted to buy a new bike offered to exchange the bike he wanted with a toy car box. The shopkeeper looks at the toy car box and says, "I would like a little more." The other boy looks at him and answers: "Take a closer look at the back of the box you have Bryan's logo, so I think you win at the change." The shopkeeper looks and answers: "Okay I accept the exchange!"

Walter was puzzled by this revelation. He couldn't believe that Bryan's items had become a form of money in this strange world of children.

He wondered what kind of society had been created in this world, where other people's toys and memories were used to buy things.

He had noticed that the children seemed to know the value of Bryan's belongings, and he wondered if they knew that these objects were actually Bryan's memories. Walter also wondered if Bryan approved of this practice.

Upon entering the small house where he had been lodged by the children, Walter saw that Bryan's belongings were scattered everywhere. He wondered if the children knew they belonged to Bryan and if they knew his story.

Leaving the house to get some fresh air, Walter walks around the city, watching the children play and run around him. He realizes that this practice of using objects as currency was more rooted in the culture of this world.

As he continued to walk, he came to a shop run by a young girl named Lucy. He notices a poster showing a shadow-shaped figure showing Bryan, without seeing his face, but just the shadow of his face. Walter wondered if Lucy knew Bryan or if she had just found this image somewhere.

Walter remembered that Jake and the others had left town, and he wondered if he should continue his investigation into this strange practice or if he should just accept it and continue his journey. But his curiosity got the better of him, and he decided to ask questions to learn more about the history of this practice.

He questioned shopkeepers and city residents about the origin of this practice, but no one seemed to know the full story. Some had heard that it started with Bryan, others thought it had always been that way. But no one seemed to know the full story.

Walter was determined to find out the truth about this strange practice, and he vows to continue investigating. He wondered what the future held for him in this strange world of children, but for now, he was happy to continue his quest for truth.

He remembered that he had always wanted to explore the world of children and understand how their society worked. Perhaps this would be his chance to unravel the mystery of this strange world.

He decided to ask Alice, the most knowledgeable person he knew in this world, to explain how Bryan's items had become currency. He knew Alice wasn't telling him everything. He had this feeling when remembering his look when Jake had spoken to him earlier. There was something that concerned her deeply, but he didn't know if it had anything to do with this bizarre society.

So he set out to find Alice, who was often difficult to locate. He had heard that she often hid in the forest near the city, so he began to look in that direction. He hoped he could find Alice and learn more about the mysteries of the children's world.

Walter drove into the forest, scanning the surroundings for Alice. He crosses the undergrowth, along streams and ponds, his curiosity grows with each step. He knew that Alice was an important figure in the city, perhaps even the most important. She was the one who had activated the practice of barter, according to rumors.

After several hours of walking, Walter finally saw a small cabin hidden under the trees. He approached cautiously and knocked on the wooden door. After a moment of waiting, the door opens to a very young girl smiling, who looks at him with a questioning look.

“Hi, I’m looking for Alice,” Walter says. “I was told that she often hid in the forest near the city. I came to ask him a few questions about Bryan’s objects and their use as currency in this strange world.”

The young lady smiled even wider. “I’m Mathilda, I’m Alice’s sister,” she says. “Welcome to my cabin. I have heard of you, Walter. You're the newcomer to our world, aren't you?"

Walter nodded, a little surprised that his arrival had already been noticed. Mathilda invites him in and offers him a cup of hot chocolate with marshmallows. They settled comfortably around the small wooden table and Walter began to ask questions about the mysteries of the children's world.

Mathilda responded patiently, explaining the history of the city and how the practice of barter was set up. She talks about Bryan and his importance to the world of children, and how the objects belonging to him had become a form of money. Walter listened carefully, taking mental notes to better understand this strange world.

Finally, after several hours of discussion, Walter got up to leave. Mathilda wished him good luck in his research and offered him a small precious object in exchange for his visit. She asks him to keep it because one day this object could help him. Walter thanked her and walked out of the cabin, delighted to have learned so much about this mysterious world. He was eager to continue his research and discover even more secrets hidden in this strange city.

After taking leave of Mathilda, Walter set out to return to the city. He reflected on everything he had learned about the world of children and was eager to share his new knowledge with other children. But along the way, he spotted a familiar figure. It was Alicc, sitting on a bench at the entrance of the city.

Walter walked over and greeted Alice, who seemed surprised to see him. He explained that he had spoken to Mathilda and learned a lot about the world of children. Alice seemed happy to see that Walter was curious and interested in learning more. She offers to accompany him for a short walk in the city.

Alice took him to a small market where the children exchanged items. She explained that this was part of the barter practice, which began with Bryan and his valuables. Walter noticed that the children looked very proud of their possessions and that they exchanged them enthusiastically.

They continued their walk through the streets of the city, stopping to chat with the children and learn more about their daily lives. Walter notes that the children were very autonomous and creative, presenting ingenious solutions to their problems. Alice explained that it was part of the children's culture and way of life.

At the end of the day, Walter thanked Alice for her company and time. He felt more connected to the children's world and applied himself better to their way of living and thinking.

After spending the day exploring the city with Alice, Walter felt more confident in his understanding of children's culture. He had learned that children were very independent and had learned to fend for themselves since they arrived in this mysterious world. He was also impressed by their creativity and ingenuity, which manifested itself in the way they solved problems and created useful objects.

During their walk, Alice introduced Walter too many children, each with their own story and way of contributing to the community. He had met children who were good gardeners, others who were good craftsmen and others who were talented musicians. Walter had been surprised by the diversity of talents and skills among the children, and he had begun to realize how rich and complex their community was.

At the end of the day, Alice had taken Walter home and given him a small precious object as a souvenir of their day together. Walter had been touched by this gesture and had promised to come back to see her soon. He was happy to have finally found a place in this mysterious world, and he was determined to continue learning more about children and their unique way of life.

Walter had noticed that something had been bothering Alice for a while now. He had asked several questions about it, but Alice had always stopped answering them directly. However, Walter couldn't help but think that something bad was going on.

One day, while walking in the children's town, Walter had mentioned Bryan and his valuables, hoping to get information about him. Alice had seemed nervous and changed the subject, but Walter had decided to persist.

"Why don't you want to talk about Bryan? Is there something wrong?" He asked.

Alice hesitated for a moment before replying, "I don't think you'll be able to meet Bryan."

"Why? What do you mean?" Walter asked, increasingly worried.

Alice looked down, as if embarrassed by what she was going to say. "The Grand Council doesn't want it!"

Walter was puzzled. "But why? What did I do?"

Alice wanted to explain that all children, once they reach the age of eighteen, had to leave the world of children and return to the world of adults. It was an immutable rule, and no one could derogate from it. But she couldn't tell Walter. Alice knew that Bryan, who several years ago had reached the fateful age of eighteen, had to leave the world of children.

Walter was puzzled. "But why doesn't the Grand Council want me to meet Bryan? What did I do?"

Alice hesitated for a moment, figuring out how to explain the situation vaguely without revealing the secret of the city's children. "It's complicated," she finally replied. "There are rules in the world of children and the Great Council makes decisions based on that. I don't know exactly why they don't want you to meet Bryan, but there must be a reason."

Walter sighed. "I don't understand. I thought we had the right to talk to whomever we wanted in this world."

Alice looked down, feeling uncomfortable lying to her friend. She wished she could explain the real reason to him, but she knew it wasn't part of the rules. "I'm sorry Walter, I can't tell you more. Maybe you should look to talk to someone else if you want to know more about Bryan."

Walter nodded, resigned. He knew something was wrong and Alice wasn't telling him everything, but he didn't want to make her uncomfortable. He was going to have to find another way to find out what was really going on in this strange world of children.

Walter couldn't help but think of Bryan and the mystery that surrounded him. He felt that something bigger was brewing behind this case and he was determined to find out more. But he also knew that he had to be careful and discreet if he wanted to avoid making Alice uncomfortable or arousing other children's suspicions.

He started asking questions of other kids he knew well, but all seemed reluctant to answer him or even talk about Bryan. This frustrated him and he began to wonder if the children of the Children's City were all involved in this conspiracy.

Despite this, Walter did not give up. He continued to search for clues and ask questions in subtle ways, hoping to uncover Alice's great secret. But as he dug deeper, he began to realize that this quest could be more dangerous than he imagined. He had noticed that some children seemed to be watching him and that his movements were increasingly limited.

Walter was beginning to get scared, but he was also curious. He felt like something important was lurking in this world of children and he couldn't stand by and do nothing. He was determined to find out the truth, even if it meant taking risks.

But Walter did not yet know that his obstinacy in discovering the truth could put him in danger. Because in this world of children, secrecy was the key to everything, and trying to unravel it risked facing the darkest consequences.

Walter had decided to conduct his own investigation to find out more about Bryan and what was going on in the world of children. He knew he had to be discreet so as not to attract the attention of other children, but his curiosity had become too great to ignore.

He had begun to observe the children around him, listening to their conversations, trying to find clues to the secrets of the city. He had even tried to talk to other children, but he couldn't find anyone who knew Bryan well or knew anything about him.

Walter had come to understand that children were as discreet as adults when it came to keeping the secrets of the city. He had almost given up on finding out the truth when something strange happened.

He had noticed strange children who seemed to follow him from a distance. They were dressed like tourists, but he had noticed that they did not take pictures or visit tourist attractions. They followed him from a distance, as if they wanted to monitor him.

Walter had begun to panic. He didn't know why young children followed him, but he felt they had discovered his curiosity about the secrets of the city. He had begun to avoid public places and only go out when he was sure he would not be followed.

He knew that if he was discovered, he could be in danger. But his curiosity was stronger than his fear. He needed to know what was being passed on to the Children's City, even if it meant putting his life at risk.

Walter walked the streets of the children's world, lost in thought. He couldn't help but think about Bryan and why the Grand Council didn't want him to meet him. He had not noticed that the children who had been following him for a while were actually members of the domestic intelligence services of the children's world.

Suddenly, a young boy named Jay approached him. "Pay attention to yourself," he whispered in Walter's ear. "They're after you."

Before Walter had time to answer, several children appeared out of nowhere and grabbed him. They quickly handcuffed him and took him to an office of the Children's World Administration.

Walter was placed in a small room with a table and chair. He was confused and scared, not knowing why he was there or what was going to happen to him. Members of the domestic intelligence services of the children's world came forward and began to interrogate him.

"It looks like you broke some rules," one of the members said. "We have received information that you are seeking to discover secrets that are forbidden in our world."

Walter tried to defend himself, but the limbs were relentless. They searched his pockets and found the notebook in which he had written his notes on the world of children. They began to flip through it, discovering information that was supposed to remain secret.

"We can't let this happen," said one of the members. "You are a danger to our world, and we must take steps to prevent you from harming our society."

Walter was dragged into a cell, with no idea what was going to happen to him. He felt like he had fallen into a trap, and he didn't know how he was going to get out of it.

Walter was sitting in his cell, recovering from the intense interrogation he had been subjected to by members of the domestic intelligence services of the children's world. He wondered what would happen to him now and if he would ever be able to get out of here.

Suddenly, he hears footsteps in the hallway and Jake entered the cell. "Hi, Walter, how's it going?" asks Jake.

Walter stood up, happy to see a familiar face. "Jake, what are you doing here?" he asks.

Jake explained that he was there to help Walter get out of prison, but that he needed his help in return. He explained that the Grand Council had discovered that Alice had spoken to Walter about Bryan, which was strictly forbidden.

They had therefore ordered Walter's arrest in order to find out if he was involved in this case.

Jake had successfully freed Walter, but in exchange, he had to promise never to reveal the secret of the town's children. "If you accept these terms, I can help you get out of here now," Jake says.

Walter hesitated for a moment, knowing that this meant refraining from his natural curiosity and desire to discover the secret of the city's children. But he also knew he had no choice if he wanted to get out of prison. "Okay, I agree.", he finally said.

Jake smiles and pulls out a key from his pocket. He unlocked the cell door and the two boys quietly left.

Walter was relieved to be free, but he was also disappointed that he had been prevented from discovering the secret of the city's children.

He wondered what was behind this mysterious organization and if he could ever learn more.

Once Jake and Walter left the prison, they began walking the silent streets of the city. Walter was grateful to Jake for helping him get out of prison, but he also felt betrayed for being forced to give up his curiosity and thirst to discover the secrets of the city's children.

Jake tried to change the subject and started talking about mundane things, but Walter was too preoccupied with recent events to be able to contain himself. Eventually, they arrived at a small park and sat on a bench to talk.

Jake explained to Walter that the children of the city had special lives in this world, but those special lives were also like a burden. The members of their organization had vowed to protect their secret at all costs, because they knew that if the outside world discovered their existence, it could put their lives at risk.

Walter listened with fascination as Jake explained more about the inner workings of the organization. Jake also promised to help Walter get out of town or the children's world if he ever decides to leave. Walter was grateful for this offer, but he knew he still had a lot to learn about the world of children.

The two boys continued to talk for hours, sharing stories and experiences. Finally, it was time for Walter to go home. Jake accompanied him to Walter's house and promised to see him again soon.

Walter entered his house, exhausted, but happy. He knew he had a lot to think about recent events, but he was also excited to discover more about the world of children. However, he knew that he had to be careful, as he had promised to keep their secret and he did not want to put their lives in danger.

6 – THE FOREST OF RIDDLES.

Walter had traveled the length and breadth of the city, looking for clues about Bryan and his connection to the town's children. But despite his efforts, he had found nothing conclusive. It was then that he remembered a place called "the forest of riddles", a mysterious and legendary place where the inhabitants of the city went to solve complex puzzles.

Walter had always been fascinated by this forest, but he had never set foot there. He knew the forest was full of traps and dangers, but he was willing to take the risk to find answers about Bryan.

Walter set out for the Riddle Forest, hoping that this place would give him clues about Bryan. He had heard about the forest many times. Along the way, he imagines solving complex puzzles and finally discovering the truth about the city's children.

When he arrived at the forest, he was struck by the mystical atmosphere there. The trees were so tall that they seemed to touch the sky, while the birds sang strange melodies in the branches. Walter felt both amazed and intimidated.

He entered the forest and began to look for clues. Walter sank into the forest of riddles, his footsteps choked by the carpet of fallen leaves beneath his feet. The towering trees formed a vault above his head, filtering out the sun's rays to create a dim light effect. He almost felt as if he had entered another world.

He walked the winding paths, looking for any trace of Bryan or the secret organization of the city's children. He looks around carefully, scanning every tree, every rock, looking for the slightest sign of activity.

After a while, he comes across a wooden panel nailed to a tree. He approached to read the inscription which read: "To find the answer, one must first solve the riddle." Walter raised his eyebrows, intrigued. It was clear that a riddle had to be solved in order to move forward.

He looked around, looking for clues, but nothing seemed to indicate a riddle. Suddenly, he heard a strange noise behind him. He turned around and saw a small animal that looked like a rat, but with a very long tail and reddish fur. The animal stared at him and made a noise that sounded like a laugh. Walter wondered if he was losing his mind. A rat with a long tail and reddish fur facing him, and even seemed to laugh at him? He couldn't believe what he saw, but he felt like this animal had something to do with the riddle he had to solve to advance through the forest.

The little animal did not move, as if expecting something from Walter. He took a deep breath and walked towards the animal, determined to find out what it would do. The rat took a step back, then made a noise that sounded like a new mockery.

Walter began to think aloud, "A riddle… Maybe this animal has something to do with the riddle I have to solve. But what?". The animal was still looking at him, with a look of defiance in his eyes. Walter suddenly felt a chill running down his back. He felt that the puzzle was much more complicated than he had initially thought.

He then began to search around, searching every nook and cranny for a clue. He didn't really know what he was looking for, but he hoped to find something that would help him solve the riddle. Finally, he notices a strange tree that stands out from the rest of the forest. On the bark there were inscriptions in the form of symbols. Walter approached the tree and began to examine the symbols.

He had no idea what that might mean, but he was convinced it was a crucial clue. It was then that he heard the strange noise behind him again. He turns around, ready to face the animal, but this time there were several animals of the same species. There were several of them staring at him, as if they were waiting for an answer.

Walter understood that the enigma may have been related to these animals. But how to understand them? He had the impression that animals had a language of their own, a language he did not know. He was determined to find the answer to this riddle, whatever the cost.

Walter began to observe the animals more closely. He noticed that their fur had strange patterns and that their tails were braided in an intricately woven way. He wondered if these motives could have any meaning if they perhaps formed some kind of code.

He pulls out a notebook from his pocket and starts drawing the patterns he sees on the animals. He thought maybe he could decipher them later. But as he was focused on his drawings, he heard a thud behind him. He turned around and saw a tree that had fallen right next to him. He had barely had time to jump to the side to avoid being crushed.

Walter understood that the forest of puzzles was not a safe place. He remembered that he had heard stories about mysterious creatures that lived in the forest, creatures that could be very dangerous if provoked. He wondered if he had done anything to annoy these strange animals.

He decides to get moving, aware that staying still could be dangerous. He treads cautiously, looking around for more clues. The animals followed him, always staring at him. Walter felt their gaze weigh on him, as if they could read his mind.

Suddenly, a heart-rending cry echoed in the forest. Walter froze, the hair on his body standing up on his skin. He had the impression that this cry was not that of an animal, but rather that of a human. He wondered whether he should continue to advance or turn back.

He then hears another cry, closer this time. He started running, hoping to find a safe place to hide. But the animals pursued him, more and more numerous. They seemed angry, as if they didn't want him to find out their secret.

Walter panicked, knowing that he had to find a solution quickly. He looked with his eyes for a way out, a way out. He then saw a hollow tree, big enough for him to hide. He rushed to the tree and rushed in, hoping that the animals would not find him.

He hid in the hollow tree for several minutes, trying to catch his breath. He could still hear the cries of the animals outside, but they seemed to be slowly moving away. He figured he was lucky not to have been caught.

Walter realized that he had made a mistake by hiding in the hollow tree. When he tried to get out, he discovered that the animals were still there, patiently waiting for him to come out of hiding. He understood then that these animals were much more intelligent than he had imagined.

He realizes that he was trapped and that he had to find another way out. He examines the hollow tree in which he is located and notices that there was a deeper cavity, hidden behind a pile of leaves and branches. He decides to slip in, hoping that the animals would not find her.

However, no sooner had he entered the cavity than he heard the animals scratching the tree. He understood that they were looking for him and that time was running out. He thought quickly and had an idea: he took out of his pocket a bar of chocolate he had on him and threw it in a direction opposite to that of the cavity.

The animals rushed to the chocolate bar, leaving Walter the opportunity to come out of hiding and run in the opposite direction. He ran as fast as he could, trying to put as much distance as possible between himself and the animals.

However, he had been so busy escaping the animals that he didn't realize he had strayed deeper into the forest. He soon finds himself facing a dangerous ravine, which seemed impossible to cross. He realized then that he was in a desperate situation, and that he had to find a solution quickly if he wanted to survive.

Walter approached the edge of the ravine and looked down. He could see the sharp rocks below, the water flowing through the rocks, and the trees hanging from the cliffside. There was no way down or down, and he felt trapped.

It was then that he remembered the legend of the "ravine of the lost children." He had heard about this story since he was in the city ruled by Alice, but he didn't know if it was true or not. Legend has it that there was a solution to cross the ravine, but that it had been kept secret for generations. Only a few chosen ones, who had managed to solve a complex riddle, had been allowed to cross the ravine safely.

Walter was determined to find the answer to the riddle. He began rummaging through his backpack, hoping to find something that could help him. It was then that he found an old card, which he had forgotten that he had taken with him. He opened it and looked carefully at the details. Suddenly, he notices a small inscription written at the bottom of the map. It was a Latin text that said, "To cross the ravine, you have to know the language of trees."

Walter didn't know how to interpret this mysterious phrase. But he was determined to solve the riddle. He spends several hours studying the forest, carefully observing each tree and plant. He wondered if there was a tree or plant that could help him understand what that phrase meant.

That's when he notices a small tree, with strange leaves and twisted branches. It looked different from other trees in the forest. Walter remembered that he had already seen this tree in books, it was a "tree of lost children", a tree that was known to be the guardian of the riddle of the ravine.

He approached the tree and began to speak in a low voice. He was trying to understand the language of the tree. He notices that the leaves moved slightly in response to his words. Walter understood then that the tree was answering him. He had finally found the key to the riddle.

He stayed with the tree for several hours, offering to understand every word and gesture. Eventually, he had solved the riddle. He knew how to cross the ravine safely.

Walter set out for the ravine, confident that he could cross it thanks to his new knowledge. But he did not know that danger awaited him on the other side of the ravine.

Walter was eager to put his acquired knowledge into practice and cross the ravine. He carefully followed the tree's instructions and finally arrived at the opposite bank, safe and sound. He was proud of himself, but also exhausted and hungry.

He looked for a safe place to rest and feed. It was then that he saw a small clearing, where he might be able to find food. But as he approaches, he notices something strange. The clearing was wrapped in strange totems, whose shapes seemed both familiar and disturbing.

Walter began to explore the totems, curious about their meaning. It was then that he heard a noise behind him. He turned to see a group of strange people, staring at him with suspicious eyes. They looked hostile and aggressive.

Walter understood then that totems and people were related, but he did not know how. He decided to stay calm and try to communicate with them, hoping they wouldn't hurt him. But he knew that if he didn't quickly find an answer to this riddle, he could be in mortal danger.

Walter put himself on the defensive, ready to defend himself, if necessary, but he first tried to calm the strange characters. He smiled softly at them, hoping it would soothe them. The people did not move, standing still, staring at him threateningly. Walter decided to take matters into his own hands and break the ice.

He took out a few items from his backpack and handed them to strangers, hoping it would make them feel more comfortable. Foreigners then began to speak a strange and incomprehensible language. Walter tried to understand what they were saying, but it was difficult, as the language seemed to be very different from anything he had heard before.

However, as he looked at the totems and listened carefully to strangers, Walter understood that the totems were actually symbols of an ancient ritual of passage. Strangers seemed to be the guardians of this ritual, responsible for ensuring that only those worthy and able to pass.

Walter then understood that if he wanted to pass, he had to go through this ritual. He asked the guards how he could pass, but they refused to answer him, claiming that only the worthy was allowed to know the ritual. Walter was determined to find a way to pass and solve the riddle.

He spends several hours studying the totems and chatting with the guardians, looking for a way to unlock the ritual. Eventually, he found a common element in the symbols and managed to decipher the ritual. The guards were impressed and decided to let him pass.

Walter passes the ritual successfully, crosses the clearing and continues his journey. But he knew he still had a lot to overcome before solving the riddle of the ravine of lost children.

After crossing the clearing, Walter finds himself in front of a large mountain. He knew that the only way to continue his journey was gravity. However, the mountain was steep and dangerous, with unstable rocks and deep crevices.

Walter began to climb the mountain, using all his climbing skills to avoid any danger. But as he was halfway up the mountain, he heard a thud behind him. As he turned around, he saw a huge avalanche coming straight down at him.

Walter ran for his life, seeking safe shelter. He found a small crevasse and took cover, just in time to avoid the avalanche. But when he tried to get out of the crevasse, he realized he was stuck. He had slipped on a loose stone and broken his ankle when he fell.

Walter was trapped in the crevasse, unable to move his broken ankle. He knew that if he didn't find help quickly, he could die of starvation or dehydration. But as he began to lose hope, he heard a familiar sound the language of the tree.

He remembered the knowledge he had gained of the clearing and the keepers and used his skills to communicate with the tree. The tree gives him advice on how to free himself and offers help to get back on his feet.

With the help of the tree, Walter managed to get out of the crevice and heal his broken ankle. He continues his journey, with a new appreciation for the wisdom of nature. However, he knew that his path was still far from over and that he had to remain vigilant in the face of the dangers that awaited him.

Walter was slowly recovering from his injury, but he knew he had to be extra vigilant if he wanted to survive in this hostile nature. He decides to take a break to recover his strength and think about his next move.

He began to evaluate his options and realized that he needed food and water to continue his journey. He remembered the clearing and the food he had found there, but he knew he couldn't go back. So he decides to look for other sources of food and water in the vicinity.

After several days of walking, Walter finally found a source of fresh water and a fertile hunting area. He began hunting and fishing for food and replenishing his water supplies. But he knew it wasn't enough to survive in the long run.

Walter then remembered the legend that several children of the city that Alice led had told him. It was the existence of a secret garden hidden in the forest, filled with food and pure water. He decides to go in search of this secret garden, hoping that he can find the resources he needed to survive.

He spends several weeks exploring the forest, looking for the secret garden. But despite his best efforts, he couldn't find it. He was about to give up when he saw a faint glow in the distance. He decided to follow the glow, which eventually led him to an enchanted clearing.

The clearing was filled with fresh fruits and vegetables, streams of pure water, and multicolored flowers. Walter felt amazed by the beauty of the place and thanked the elderly for their wisdom of nature. He spends several days in the secret garden, feeding and resting. But he knew that his journey was not yet over and that he had to continue to advance towards his ultimate goal, solving the riddle of Bryan's existence.

After regaining strength in the secret garden, Walter was ready to continue his journey. He remembered the clues he had required and began to ponder the riddle of Bryan's existence. He realizes that he needed more information to be able to solve the mystery.

He decides to seek help from the inhabitants of the forest and participates in the search for the tribe of Sages. After several days of walking, he finally found the hidden village of the Sages.

Walter explained his quest to the Sages and asked for their help in finding information about Bryan's existence. The Sages were impressed by Walter's determination and decided to help him.

They spent days studying ancient scrolls and sacred texts, looking for answers to the riddle.

Eventually, they found a legend that told the story of Bryan, the son of a legendary explorer who had traveled with his father to the forbidden lands and discovered a secret that would have changed the world forever.

Walter was delighted to have found this information and thanked the Sages for their help. He now knew that he had to go in search of the forbidden lands to find answers to Bryan's riddle. But he also knew that forbidden lands were a dangerous place, full of perils and obstacles. He had to be ready for any challenge that came his way.

Walter set out for the forbidden lands, aware of the dangers that awaited him. He spends weeks traversing difficult terrain, battling storms and extreme temperatures. Despite the difficulties, he continued to move forward, determined to find the answers to Bryan's riddle.

Finally, he arrived on the outskirts of the forbidden lands. He knew the dangers would be even greater inside, but he was willing to take the risk. He enters the forbidden lands and begins to explore the area, looking for signs of Bryan.

After a few days, he stumbled upon the ruins of an ancient city, which had been abandoned for several years now. Walter knew he was on the right track because this city had been built by Bryan. Walter knew this because Bryan's emblem could be seen in various parts of this secret city. He began exploring the ruins, looking for clues to Bryan's life and the secret he had discovered.

After a few days, Walter stumbles upon a secret chamber hidden behind a wall. Inside the room, he found a diary belonging to Bryan, in which he had recorded his discoveries and adventures. Walter was captivated by Bryan's writing and began to read carefully.

Walter was completely captivated by reading Bryan's diary, devouring every word excitedly. He was fascinated by Bryan's adventures and discoveries and learned more about the secret he had discovered. However, there was one phrase that baffled him: "We are many." Walter had no understanding of what that meant. Who was the other Bryan was talking about? Were they explorers, scientists, or mystical creatures? Walter felt like there was another dimension to Bryan's story, but he couldn't grasp the meaning.

He rereads the passage several times, looking for clues and leads. He wondered if this riddle had anything to do with the secret Bryan had uncovered. He was determined to understand this mystery and solve it, but he didn't know where to start.

Walter was overcome with conflicting emotions. On the one hand, he was thrilled to have found Bryan's diary and to discover important information about his trip. But on the other side, he was frustrated that he didn't understand this mysterious phrase. He felt like he was missing an essential piece of the puzzle, and it puzzled him.

Walter knew he had to keep looking for answers, even if he didn't know where it would take him. He takes Bryan's diary and neatly stores it in his bag. He stood up, determined to continue his exploration of the ruins, and discover Bryan's secret, whatever it may be.

Walter continued his search in the ruins of the abandoned city. He knew he had to find answers to his questions, even if it meant spending several days exploring.

After a few hours, he entered a strange room, decorated with enigmatic drawings on the walls. He was fascinated by the patterns and symbols that seemed to have been carved into stone for several years. But it was next to a drawing that he saw something that made him shudder enigmatic sentences, written in red letters: "We form one" and "With several we are one."

Walter was shocked and excited at the same time. These sentences reminded him of the mysterious phrase in Bryan's diary, "There are many of us." It was clear that these messages were linked in some way. But what did that mean?

Walter began to study the drawings and messages carefully. He tried to decipher the symbols and patterns, looking for clues to Bryan's secret and the others he had talked about. But the more he studied the drawings, the more lost he felt. The symbols seemed meaningless, and the messages were as cryptic as ever.

Walter took a break and thought about the situation. It was obvious that he could not solve this mystery alone. He needed help, an ally who could help him understand the meaning of these messages. But who? He was alone in the abandoned city, without any contact with the outside world.

Walter knew he had to find a solution, but he didn't know where to start. He sat on the floor, lost in thought, looking for a solution to his problem. He felt that time passed slowly, that every minute was an eternal moment of reflection.

However, despite his discouragement, Walter could not give up. He knew he had to keep looking for answers, even if it meant confronting unknown dangers. He got up and set out to find a way to unravel Bryan's secret.

After hours of fruitless searching, Walter was about to give up his quest to understand the mystery of the cryptic messages. Night had fallen, and the room was plunged into darkness. He is about to go out to find a safe place to spend the night when he notices a slight flicker on one of the drawings.

Intrigued, Walter approached the drawing and realized that a new message had been engraved next to the drawing. He read aloud, "At the Crystal Labyrinth, part of the secret will be revealed." Walter was amazed and at the same time delighted by this discovery. He now had a new clue to follow.

He immediately set out to find this Crystal Labyrinth, without knowing exactly where it was. He knew that he had to take risks to find answers, and that the road would be fraught with pitfalls. He will remember Bryan's diary, hoping to find a clue that could help him find the way.

As he walked in the dark, Walter pondered what this Crystal Labyrinth could be. He remembered that Bryan had mentioned a legendary city in the heart of the forest, a city full of traps and secrets. Maybe it was there that he would find this famous Crystal Labyrinth.

Walter continued on his way, keeping this in mind, concentrating on the mission ahead. He was determined to find answers, no matter what, and to uncover Bryan's secret.

7 – THE CRYSTAL LABYRINTH.

After discovering the new riddle inscribed on the drawings, Walter decided: he had to find the famous Crystal Labyrinth. After gathering his belongings and taking one last sip of water, he set out to reach his goal.

The journey was difficult. Walter had had to walk for several hours through steep and hostile terrain, jumping over dangerous rocks and crevices. He had followed an ancient stone path, which had been overgrown. At times, he had to make his way through thorny bushes that lacerated his clothes.

Finally, he had arrived at the entrance of the crystal labyrinth. The site was hidden behind a thick layer of mist, which made it almost invisible. Walter had to move carefully, groping through the mist until he could see the contours of the labyrinth.

The Crystal Labyrinth was a true masterpiece. Each wall was made of sparkling crystal, which shone under the sun's rays. The whole structure seemed to vibrate with a mysterious energy, which presented Walter with chills in the back.

Walter had begun to advance through the labyrinth, following the tortuous path that would lead him to Bryan's supposed revelation. But the route was complex, with crystal walls that seemed to change shape and color with each step. The crossings were narrow and winding, and the intersections were numerous.

He had continued to move forward, sometimes getting lost in the alleys of the maze, but never losing sight of his goal. The name of the labyrinth came from the fact that the walls seemed to be composed of colored crystals, which cast shimmering reflections with each movement of Walter. He felt like he was inside a giant kaleidoscope.

As he progressed, Walter began to notice strange drawings on the crystal walls. They seemed to be symbolic representations of an ancient language, which must have been used by the inhabitants of the abandoned city. Walter had tried to decipher them, but they seemed as cryptic as the previous messages.

Despite the difficulties, Walter had persevered, slowly moving through the labyrinth. Finally, after several hours of wandering through the winding corridors, he had arrived at a central hall.

In the center of the room was a kind of pedestal, on which was placed a shiny object. It was a small crystal sphere, which emitted a soft and warm light. Walter approached and saw that the object was engraved with strange symbols. He knew this was the key to unraveling Bryan's mystery.

Walter was amazed to hear a voice speak to him while he was alone in the room. He looked around, tried to understand where the voice was coming from. Finally, his eyes landed on the crystal sphere he was holding in his hand.

He looked at the sphere, tried to understand what is transmitted. The voice spoke again, this time louder and clearer: "I am the soul of the Crystal Labyrinth. What is your question?"

Walter was shocked. He didn't know what to say. After a moment of silence, he replied, "I'm looking for Bryan's secret. I am here to unravel the mystery of his life."

The voice in the crystal sphere replied in a soft but firm tone: "Bryan's secret cannot be found here, Walter. But I can help you find what you're looking for if you're up for the challenge."

Walter nodded, curious to know what was in store for him. The voice continued, "You have to go through three tests to find what you're looking for. The first is to find the Hall of Mirrors, where you will have to confront your own image. The second test will take you to the Garden of Illusions, where you will have to find your way through deceptive illusions. The final trial will take you into darkness, where you will have to face your deepest fears."

Walter was taken aback. He hadn't planned to face trials of this nature, but he was determined to find Bryan's secret. He accepted the conditions set by the entity of the crystal sphere and began to prepare for the tests.

The voice added before disappearing: "Be prepared, Walter. The trials await you."

Walter found himself alone in the room, a small crystal sphere in his hand, wondering what awaited him in the next trials.

Walter got up and began to explore the corridors of the Crystal Labyrinth. He walked for a while, not knowing where he was going. The walls were made of sparkling crystals, which projected light reflections in all directions. Silence reigned, and Walter heard only the sound of his own footsteps.

After a while, he was faced with a choice of a path. There were two corridors open to him, and he didn't know which one to take. He looked at the crystal sphere in his hand, hoping it could help him, but she didn't seem to say anything. Finally, he chose the right lane and continued to move forward.

After a while, Walter began to notice changes in the environment. The walls seemed darker, and the crystals were dying out one after the other. The floor was covered with moss, and cobwebs hung from the ceiling. Walter began to feel more and more uncomfortable, as if something sinister was lurking in the darkness.

Suddenly, he heard a noise. It was a squeak, as if something metallic rubbed against a rough surface. Walter slowed down, worried, and began to listen. The noise continued, louder and louder, until it became deafening. Walter began to panic, wondering what could possibly make such a noise.

Suddenly, a door opened in front of him, and Walter was thrown into a circular room. He landed on the ground, shaken and disoriented. He stood up, trying to understand what had just happened, and looked around. The walls were covered with mirrors, which reflected his image ad infinitum.

Walter understood that he had reached the Hall of Mirrors, but he did not know what he had to do. He tried to touch the mirrors, but they seemed untouchable. He looked at his clean reflection, which looked at him with intensity. The mirrors seemed to speak to him, taught him, challenge him.

Walter began to feel more and more uncomfortable. He felt like the mirrors were trying to tell him something, but he couldn't explain why. He tried to leave but realized that all the doors were blocked. He was stuck in the Hall of Mirrors, with only his own reflection as his companion.

Walter began to panic, realizing that he had fallen into the trap of the first test. He had to find a way out of this room before the mirrors drove him crazy.

Walter approached one of the mirrors, fascinated by the image that reflected it. But suddenly, he noticed that something was wrong. The image of his reflection seemed to become blurred and independent of his movements. He blinked, thinking that it was just his imagination playing tricks on him, but when he opened his eyes again, the image had changed.

He saw a version of himself in a hospital bed, surrounded by his parents who seemed worried. Then the image changed, and he saw himself playing with his dog in a park, happy and carefree. But then the image took a strange turn. He saw images of him arguing with his friends, failing his exams, losing his job as a newspaper delivery man, sinking into depression.

Walter began to panic, realizing that the mirrors showed him scenes from his life that he would have preferred to forget and other passages that he did not know as if the mirrors could imagine the future. He tried to move away from the mirrors, but he was trapped, unable to turn away from the image that fascinated and terrified him at the same time.

The images continued to scroll before his eyes, increasingly dark and despairing. Walter felt as if his worst nightmares were coming to life in front of him, and he couldn't get rid of them. He started screaming, crying, asking the mirrors to stop.

Suddenly, a voice echoed through the room, soft but firm: "You have to face your past, your present and your future potential, Walter. You have to accept your mistakes and learn to live with them. Otherwise, you will be a prisoner of your own regrets forever."

The images began to dissolve, and Walter saw his own reflection looking at him compassionately. He realized that the first test was designed to face his own inner demons, and that he had to learn to defeat them in order to move forward. With this realization, the doors of the Hall of Mirrors were unlocked, allowing Walter to move on to the second test.

Walter walked out of the Hall of Mirrors, still trembling, and shaken by the images he had seen. He found himself in a dark, narrow corridor, stretching as far as the eye could see in both directions. He looked around, looking for a sign to know where to go next, but all he could see was darkness.

Walter began to move slowly, trying not to trip or fall. He heard strange noises that seemed to come from nowhere and everywhere at the same time. Whispers, laughter, screams, tears. They were so numerous and so different that Walter could not distinguish them from each other.

The further he went, the narrower the corridor became, until it was almost impossible to breathe. Walter felt like he was locked in an endless tunnel, and he didn't know if he could continue.

Suddenly, a door appeared in front of him, illuminated with a strange blue light. Walter was relieved to see a way out of this nightmare, but he was also worried about what was behind the door.

He pushed open the door, and he found himself in a beautiful garden, with flowers of all colors and shapes. But something was wrong. The flowers moved, twisted, changed color, as if they were alive and conscious.

Walter tread carefully, trying not to touch the flowers, but it was clear that they were there to scare him. The flowers began to turn into strange and scary things, snakes, spiders, clawed hands, sharp teeth. Walter started running, but the flowers seemed to tighten around him, as if he was trapped in a giant spider web.

He kept running, looking for a way out of the garden, but he was as if trapped in a plant maze. The flowers kept turning into more and more frightening shapes, and Walter felt like they were following him, chasing him away.

Finally, Walter managed to find the exit from the Garden of Illusions. He was exhausted, traumatized, and scared, but he knew he had to keep moving forward if he wanted to reach the end of his ordeal.

After leaving the Garden of Illusions, Walter finds himself in a dark and narrow corridor. The walls appeared to be made of rough stone and the torches associated with the walls gave a faint reddish glow that illuminated only the nearest areas. Walter tread cautiously, not knowing what awaited him beyond the darkness.

At the end of the hallway, he arrived in a strange room. There was nothing but a wooden chair, placed in the middle of the room, with a small table next to it. On the table was a lit candle that projected a dim light into the room. Walter wondered what to do.

Suddenly, the candle went out, plunging the room into darkness. Murmurs were heard in the darkness, followed by diabolical laughter. Walter felt a cold hand land on his shoulder, and he screamed in terror. The hand pushed him hard towards the chair, forcing him to sit down.

A sinister voice was heard then, echoing through the room: "Walter, you are now facing your deepest fears. You have to face them if you want to survive. You have made mistakes in your life, mistakes that have haunted you for a long time. Now you have to face these mistakes, face them, accept them and finally, let them go."

The whispers and diabolical laughter reproduce, but this time Walter did not panic. He knew he had to face his fears if he wanted to get out of this ordeal. He closed his eyes, took a deep breath, and began to reflect on his past mistakes.

He remembered a time when he had been grueling to a friend, another when he had lied to his parents, and yet another when he had been selfish. The images scrolled in his head, more and more lively and realistic. He could feel the pain of his friends and family, the shame and regret overwhelming him.

Suddenly, the room lights up again, revealing a door that wasn't there before. Walter understood that this was the way out, but he knew that he had to face his fears first. He focuses on his past mistakes, accepts that they exist and that he had to learn from them. He then felt warmth invade his body and a feeling of relaxation overwhelmed him.

He got up from the chair, opened the door, and found himself in a room even darker than the previous one. Footsteps were heard, but he couldn't see who or what was doing them. He knew he had to keep moving forward, despite the fear that invaded him.

Walter walked cautiously into the dark room, relying on footsteps for guidance. The atmosphere was oppressive, as if something evil was hovering in the air. He heard whispers, laughter, and screams, which seemed to come closer to him. He tried to reason with himself by telling himself that they were only hallucinations, but that the sounds were real.

He arrives at a turning point and sees a dark figure looming in front of him. He couldn't tell what it was, but he felt something was wrong. The figure began to approach him, and Walter could soon see that it was a deformed creature, with sharp claws and sharp teeth.

Walter tried to back off, but he stumbled and fell to the hard ground. The creature moved closer to him, its claws sparkling in the faint glow of the room. Walter closed his eyes, knowing it was too late to flee. He accepted his fate, convinced that it was his punishment for all the mistakes he had made in the past.

Suddenly, he heard a familiar voice, that of his deceased grandfather. The voice was soft and reassuring, and she told him not to be afraid that everything would be fine. Walter remembered the time he had spent with his grandfather, his wisdom and kindness. He also remembered the teachings his grandfather had given him about courage and resilience.

He opened his eyes again, and the creature was gone. He suddenly felt stronger, braver. He understood that the creature was his own fear, his own inner monster. He realized that if he accepted his mistakes and weaknesses, he could overcome his fears.

He walked into the dark room, the footsteps fading little by little. He finally arrives at a door, which opens onto a room dazzling with light. Walter was happy and free from his fears.

The ordeal was finally over, and Walter understood that this adventure had changed him profoundly. He had learned to accept his mistakes, face his fears, and forgive himself. He was ready to face life's challenges with courage and determination, thanks to the teachings that trials had given him.

In the dazzling room of light, Walter saw a 13-year-old boy, Sam, standing in the center of the room. Sam had black hair in battle that fell down his forehead and framed his face. He had lightly tanned skin, piercing green eyes and a warm smile.

Sam wore a black t-shirt with white geometric patterns, dark jeans, and black and white sneakers. He looked comfortable in his clothes and confident in his gait.

Walter walked up to Sam and said, "Hi, I'm Walter. How did you get here?" Sam smiled and replied, "Hi, Walter, my name is Sam. I came here like you, looking for something. And you, what brought you here?"

Walter briefly explained his journey and personal quest, then asked Sam if he had any information about where they stood out. Sam mysteriously replied, "I might have important information for you, but before that, you have to answer a question for me. What is your biggest fear?"

Walter hesitated for a moment, then remembered what he had learned in his previous test. He decided to face his fear and replied, "My biggest fear is that I will never be able to be the person I want to be, that I will never find my place in this world."

Sam nodded, as if he had gotten the answer he was waiting for. He then said, "I think I can help you find what you're looking for, but for that, you have to follow me." He turns and walks towards a door that mysteriously opens as he approaches. Walter decided to follow him, intrigued by this mysterious boy and his promises of help.

Walter followed Sam through the mysterious door that opened at his approach, curious to find out what he had in store for him. The room in which they stood out was dark, but Walter could feel a strange energy reigning there. He turns to Sam and asks, "What's going on here? Why is it so dark?"

Sam smiled and replied mysteriously, "You'll find out soon, Walter. But before that, I need to ask you another question. What are you really looking for? What motivates him to continue?"

Walter thought for a moment before answering, "I'm trying to find my place in this world, to understand who I really am and what I want to do with my life. But what motivates me the most is knowing that I can overcome my personal fears and challenges to achieve my goals."

Sam nodded, apparently satisfied with the answer. He approached Walter and put his hand on his shoulder. "I can help you achieve your goals, Walter. But for that, you have to show courage and self-confidence. Are you up for the challenge?"

Walter looked Sam straight in the eye and nodded, determined to find out what this strange boy had in store for him. He felt both excited and anxious about what lay ahead, but he was determined to overcome any challenges that came his way.

Their conversation had created an atmosphere of mutual trust and mutual support, and Walter felt comfortable in Sam's presence. He was curious to find out where this adventure would take him and how Sam would help him achieve his goals.

Sam looks Walter straight in the eye and smiles. "All right, Walter. You're up for the challenge, it's perfect. Follow me and do whatever I tell you, no questions asked. Are you ready?"

Walter nodded, ready to follow Sam wherever he went. He was confident in himself and his ability to help him achieve his goals.

Sam opened another door that led to a spiral staircase down to the basement. They began to descend the steps, in silence. The light was dimming more and more, but Walter could still feel this strange energy hovering in the air.

After an endless descent, they finally arrived at the basement. The room was smaller than the previous one, but just as dark. Walter could hear strange noises coming from the other end of the room.

Sam turned to Walter and said, "Now you're going to have to be brave, Walter. I'm going to ask you to walk to the other end of the room, where there is a box. You have to open it and take what's inside. Are you ready?"

Walter nodded, fear beginning to take hold of him. He didn't know what awaited him, but he was determined to overcome all obstacles.

He walked slowly towards the box, the strange noises getting louder and louder. He opened the box and discovered a key inside.

"Take the key, Walter," Sam said. "This key will open the door to your goal. But for that, you have to conquer your greatest fear. Are you ready?"

Walter looked at the key in his hand, hesitating. But he remembered his determination to conquer his fears and replied, "Yes, I'm ready."

Sam smiled at her. "Very good. Now, follow me."

Walter followed Sam through another door leading to an even darker room. He could barely see where he was going, but he could hear strange noises around him. Sam asked him to stand ready as he lit a small torch, illuminating the room.

The room was small and dark, but there was a large metal door looked at the bottom. Sam told Walter that the key he had taken from the box would open that door, but before that, he had to face his biggest fear.

Walter hesitated, not knowing how he would overcome his greatest fear. Sam noticed her nervousness and told her that he just had to focus on his goal and overcome his fear in order to use the key.

Sam took out a small box from his pocket and opened it, revealing a spider. Walter jumped, knowing that his biggest fear was spiders. Sam explained that in order to use the key, he had to hold the spider in his hand without letting go until he reached the door.

Walter hesitated for a moment, but he knew he had to overcome his fear to achieve his goal. He took the spider in his trembling hand and began to walk towards the metal door. Every step was difficult, but Walter kept moving forward despite the fear growing inside him.

Finally, he arrived at the door and inserted the key. The door opened slowly, revealing a bright and spacious room. Walter looked around, amazed by the beauty of the room.

Sam smiled and said, "Congratulations, Walter. You have overcome your greatest fear and you have achieved your goal. Now you can move forward and find your place in this world."

Walter felt a sense of pride and satisfaction come over him. He knew it wasn't going to be easy, but he was confident in himself and his ability to overcome the obstacles that stood in front of him. He was ready to face whatever came his way to achieve his dreams.

8 – REVELATION.

Walter had spent the last few days thinking about the meaning of his experience with Sam. He had finally managed to achieve his greatest fear and had achieved his goal. Now he sought to go further, to understand the mysteries that surrounded him.

One day, while he was sitting in his room, Sam came to see him. "Walter, I was wondering if you weren't looking for information about Bryan," Sam said. Walter was surprised, not knowing how to comment Sam had been able to guess his innermost thoughts.

Finally, Walter confessed the truth: he wanted to know who Bryan really was. Sam smiled and said, “I think I can help you with this. Follow me.”

Sam led Walter to a park, where they settled on a bench. Sam took out a small notebook from his pocket and started writing something. He handed the notebook to Walter.

“These are the names of the five boys who run the land of children together. They all have different personalities and are very strong in their own way. Bryan is just a legend, a myth. He is the imaginary symbol of his five boys. An old memory. He was the very first child in our world. Bryan was named leader of our world. But you know no one is eternal. Bryan was our leader, but he would be nothing without the others. Because it is his boys who keep his memory, his past, his present and his future alive. In fact, Bryan is the name of the band that runs our world. You must have heard of the Great Council? Well, the Bryan group or the Grand Council is one and only group. They are very powerful, but they are also very dangerous. Be careful, Walter.", Sam warned.

Walter looked at the names written on the paper, wondering who these boys were and what role they played in his life. He now knew that the truth was far more complex than he imagined.

Sam smiled at her and said, "I'm here if you need me, Walter. Don't forget that you've already found your biggest fear. You can overcome anything that comes your way."

Walter nodded, grateful to Sam for his help. He knew the road ahead would be difficult, but he felt more confident now that he had important information about Bryan and his associates. He was ready to discover the truth and face any challenges that came his way.

Walter took the little notebook carefully and put it in his pocket. He felt both shaken and liberated by Sam's revelations. Everything he thought he knew about Bryan was wrong, and now he had to relearn everything.

He thanked Sam for his help and started walking towards the exit of the park. But as he was about to leave, something caught his eye. In the distance, he saw a group of boys playing a game. They were laughing and having fun, but something intriguing about their attitude caught Walter's attention.

He began to walk towards them, intrigued. As he got closer, he was able to make out the five boys who were on Sam's list. They were younger than he had imagined, probably his age. But he could feel their power and influence miles away.

Walter stopped a few meters away from them, observers. He noticed that each of the boys had a different role to play in the group. One of them was clearly the leader, with a natural authority that drew others to him. Another was quieter and reserved, but Walter could see the strength of character in his eyes.

He understood that these boys were the true masters of the children's world, the guardians of order and balance. They were the guarantors of peace and security, but also the guardians of truth.

Walter approached them, his heart pounding. He knew it was dangerous, but he was determined to find out the truth about Bryan and his role in the world of children.

The leader of the group turned to him, the attentive observer. Walter mustered up the courage and said, "I want to know the truth about Bryan and the Great Council. I'm ready to learn everything. "

The boys exchanged glances, but no one said anything for a while. Finally, the leader nodded and said, "All right, Walter. You have proven your determination and will. We're going to tell you everything you want to know. But now that the truth can be hard to hear. Are you ready for this?"

Walter took a deep breath and replied, "I'm ready for anything."

The five boys took Walter to a small clearing away from prying eyes. They sat in a circle, and the leader began to tell the story of Bryan and the Great Council.

"Bryan was a kid like you, Walter. He was the first child to be born into our world, and he had a special gift. He was endowed with great wisdom and had a keen authorized mind. The other children looked at him with admiration and considered him their natural leader. But Bryan didn't want to be their boss. He wanted something bigger, something that would transcend their small community of children.

That's when he had an amazing idea. He created the Great Council, a group of five children who would rule the world of children together. Each member of the Council would have a specific task to accomplish for the good of the community. The Council would be responsible for security, justice, and truth. And Bryan would be their leader, guide, and mentor.

Initially, the Council worked well. The five members worked together to maintain peace and harmony in the world of children. But over time, they began to argue and quarrel over how best to govern. Differences of opinion have led to tensions and conflicts, and the Council has begun to disintegrate.

Bryan tried to keep the group together, but it was too late. The other members of the Council had already distanced themselves, each seeking to establish its own power and control. Bryan died soon after, left behind a divided children's world plagued by confusion and chaos.

In the process, Council members were replaced by other children, each seeking to establish their own authority and power. But there has never been a leader as great as Bryan. That is why his name has remained associated with the whole group, although the Grand Council is the real power in place.

It's a very secretive and powerful organization, Walter. They have informants in every nook and cranny of our world. They know everything that is happening and everything that is being said. And they do not tolerate traitors or dissidents. "

Walter listened carefully, now understanding what was at stake. He realized that his desire to discover the truth could put him in danger, but he was determined to continue his quest.

"I'm ready to deal with all of this," he says. But how can I find the truth about Bryan and the Great Council?"

The leader thought for a moment before answering, "There is only one way to find out the truth, Walter. You must draw near to the Great Council and gain their trust. But be careful, they are very cunning and very dangerous. Never let your guard down, and never believe everything they say."

Walter doesn't understand. He thought of the five children in front of him were members of the Grand Council or group named after Bryan. Intrigued, Walter asks them: "Aren't You the Grand Council?"

The most silent and reserved replied to Walter: "No, you were talking to one of them in a very short time ago. That's why your question surprised us!"

Walter was stunned, Sam he trusted lied to him and him himself is a member of the Grand Council of the Children's World and the Bryan Group. Walter said aloud, "Sam lied to me!"

"Who is Sam?" asks one of the other boys. Walter replied, "The boy I was chatting with on the bench." The boy retorts to Walter in a mocking tone: "His name is not Sam, it's Yann. This is Bryan's 'Y'. It's like Alice who is Bryan's 'A'."

After having Yann's true identity and realizing that he was part of the Grand Council, Walter was even more determined to uncover the truth about Bryan and the secret organization. He decides to follow the leader's advice and approach the Grand Council to gain their trust.

Walter began to spend more time in the world of children, looking for opportunities to meet members of the Great Council. He also sought to learn more about Bryan and how he created the Grand Council. He spent hours reading books on children's history and interviewing elderly people who knew Bryan.

Walter had more and more doubts about the members of the Great Council, he knew that this organization had agents everywhere and that they could be dangerous if they discovered its intentions. He remembered Jake, the man who got him out of prison following his arrest by Domestic Intelligence. Jake had no trouble getting Walter out of prison. Now Walter wondered if he was one of the members of the Great Council.

Walter began investigating Jake in secret, looking into whether he had any ties to the Grand Council or to “Bryan”. He used every resource at his disposal to gather information about Jake.

He began by digging through the city’s archives for information about Jake. He discovered that he had worked for the city’s security services for several years before joining the Central Directorate of Internal Security. This aroused Walter’s suspicions, because he knew that the Directorate of Internal Security was often in contact with the Grand Council and that it was, they who headed the Internal Security Service.

Walter continued his investigation of Jake by interviewing Jake’s former colleagues. He learned that Jake was considered an exceptional agent, able to solve the most complex cases. However, he also had a reputation for being extremely secretive and reserved.

Walter continued his investigations by digging through the archives of the Central Directorate of Homeland Security, hoping to find evidence of Jake's participation in the Grand Council or the Bryan group. However, he was surprised to discover that Jake had no direct ties to these secret organizations.

This led Walter to wonder why Jake had decided to get him out of prison. Was it just an act of kindness or was there a deeper reason behind it?

Walter finally decided to confront Jake and ask him why he got him out of prison. He needed clear and direct answers to move forward with his investigation. After stalking Jake for several days, he finally found him in a small café outside the city.

"Walter! It's a surprise to see you here," Jake said as he saw Walter approaching his table.

"I'm sorry to bother you, Jake. I need to ask you a question," Walter replied.

"I'm listening," Jake said, taking a sip of his coffee.

"Why did you get me out of prison?" asks Walter directly.

Jake took a deep breath before responding. "It was at the request of Mathilda, Alice's sister."

"Alice? You mean the member of the Grand Council?" Walter exclaimed, incredulous.

Jake nodded. "Yes, Alice is a very influential member of the Grand Council. And Mathilda is my girlfriend. She heard about you and your situation, and she insisted that I help you."

Walter was stunned. He found it hard to believe that Mathilda and Jake were involved with the Grand Council. "Why did Mathilda want you to help me?" he asks.

"She just wanted to give you a chance to prove your worth," Jake replied. "She believed in you, Walter. And she had hoped that you could be an asset to the Great Council."

Walter thought for a moment. He knew that the members of the Grand Council were very suspicious and did not let anyone join their ranks. But he couldn't help but wonder if Mathilda had deeper motives.

"That explains why you got me out of prison, but it doesn't answer all my questions," Walter says. "I want to know if you're involved with the Grand Council or with Bryan."

Jake shook his head. "No, I'm not involved with them. I simply work for the Central Directorate of Internal Security. But I can't say more, Walter. If Alice finds out I'm talking to you, I'll be in big trouble."

Walter understood that Jake was sincere in his answers, but he still had many doubts about

Mathilda's and the Grand Council's motives. He needed to continue investigating to find out the truth about this secret organization. "Thank you for your answers, Jake. I'll leave you alone now."

Jake nodded. "Watch out for yourself, Walter. The Great Council can be dangerous if you try too hard to discover them."

After leaving the café, Walter walked to his house, reflecting on the conversation he had had with Jake. He was always concerned about the intentions of the Grand Council and Alice's sister Mathilda. As he opened the door of his car, he heard a familiar voice behind him.

"Walter!"

Walter turned around and saw Alice's loyal friend Elliot approaching him. Elliot had always been a bit of a mystery and had never been directly involved in the affairs of the Grand Council, but Walter knew he was very close to Alice.

"Elliot! What are you doing here?" Walter asked.

Elliot smiled. "I came to get you. Alice wants to see you."

Walter frowned. "Alice? What for?"

Elliot shrugged. "I don't know. She wouldn't tell me. But she insisted that I find you and take you home. Are you coming?"

Walter hesitated. He was curious to know what Alice wanted, but he was also aware of the risks he ran by approaching the Great Council. In the end, his curiosity outweighs his caution.

"Okay, I'm coming with you," he said.

Elliot motioned for him to follow him and led Walter through the streets of town. They eventually arrived in front of a large stone house with Doric columns. Elliot brought Walter and made him wait in the living room.

Walter waited impatiently and apprehensively. He didn't know what to expect, but he knew it wasn't going to be easy. Finally, Alice enters the room.

"Walter," she said, holding out her hand. "I'm glad you came."

Walter shook Alice's hand. "What's going on, Alice? Why did you bring me here?"

Alice turns to Elliot. "Thank you, Elliot. You can leave us now."

Elliot nodded and walked out of the room. Alice sat across from Walter and took a deep breath.

"I wanted to tell you about your investigation of the Great Council", she said.

Walter tensed. "What do you know?"

Alice looked down. "I know you have doubts about us. And I wanted to tell you that you are right to be suspicious. The Grand Council is a dangerous organization, Walter. We have enemies everywhere. We must be vigilant if we are to survive."

Walter was surprised by Alice's sincerity. He had always regarded the members of the Great Council as unscrupulous conspirators, but Alice seemed genuinely concerned.

"What do you mean?" he asks.

Alice took a deep breath. "I mean I'm not an enemy, Walter. I want to help you return home, to your home world."

Walter looks at Alice with a mixture of surprise and hope. “How can you help me go back to my home world?” he asks.

Alice smiled softly at him. “Maybe I have a way to do that. But for that, I need your help.”

Walter straightened up in his chair, interested. “What do you need?”

“I have to retrieve something that belonged to Bryan,” Alice says. “It’s been lost for years, but I think I know where to find it. If I manage to get my hands on it, maybe I could use it to send you back to your world.”

“And how can I help you?” asked Walter.

Alice looked down. “This is where it gets complicated, Walter. If I want to recover this item, I will have to go through illegal channels. I can’t go alone. I need someone I trust, someone who can help me discreetly.”

Walter immediately understood what Alice was getting at. "You want me to help you steal this item?"

Alice nodded. "I know it sounds crazy, but I have no other choice. And if you help me, I promise to do everything to get you home."

Walter thought for a moment. He knew it was dangerous, but he really wanted to go home. "Okay," he finally said. "I'll help you. But you have to promise me that you will do everything you can to help me afterwards. And that you will tell me everything you know about the Great Council."

Alice nodded. "I promise you I'll do everything I can to help you. But you must also promise me not to look for more information about the Great Council. It's too dangerous, Walter."

Walter hesitated for a moment. He was still determined to find out the truth about the Great Council, but he knew he couldn't do it alone. "Okay," he finally said. "I promise not to look for more information about the Grand Council. But you have to promise to help me as much as possible."

Alice smiled at him. "I promise you, Walter. Now we need to start planning our plan to retrieve this item from Bryan."

Alice took a deep breath before continuing: "The object we are looking for is in the city called "The City of Brigands". It is a dangerous and illegal place where all kinds of criminals gather. But I know that the object is on a black-market stall in this city."

Walter frowned. "How are we going to get there? And how are we going to find the spread on the black market?"

Alice smiled. "We're going to have to use false identities and blend in. I know how we can get those identities and how we can get into the city without arousing suspicion. As for the black-market stall, we will have to ask questions and find contacts in the city. But I'm sure we'll get there."

Walter nodded. "Okay. But I'm not sure I can handle the violence and crime in this city."

Alice put a hand on Walter's shoulder. "Don't worry, Walter. We will be together, and we will protect each other. And if all goes well and we will be back quickly. And then I promise to do everything I can so that you can go back to the world where you came from."

Walter felt reassured by Alice's words. "Okay, I'm willing to try. But we have to be careful and not get caught."

Alice nodded. 'Absolutely. We must be careful and discreet at every stage of our journey.

She stood up and held out her hand to Walter. "Let's go, Walter. We have work to do."

Alice and Walter had decided to go to the City of Brigands to retrieve Bryan's item from a black-market stall. They knew it was a risky trip and they had to be careful. So they began to prepare their trip carefully.

First, Alice searched for information about the city of brigands, using her contacts to get an idea of the current situation of the city. She discovered that the city was dangerous, and that violence was common. She also learned that the townspeople were suspicious of outsiders, which meant they had to find a way to get through the glimpses.

Alice then found a contact who could provide them with false identities to allow them to pass through the previews. She also bought clothes and accessories to help them blend in with the crowd. She chose simple and discreet clothes, which would not make them notice. Walter was also equipped with a small knife in case they needed to defend themselves.

Then, Alice programmed their route to get to the city. She chose a path that avoided the main roads, as they were often controlled by bandits. So they decided to cross the forest and follow the small trails. Alice also planned to hide in the forest if necessary and use the bypass roads if the main roads were blocked.

After preparing their itinerary, Alice and Walter began packing their bags for their trip. They brought supplies for a few days, as well as useful tools such as a compass, flashlight and matches. Alice also provided a small first-aid kit, with medication and bandages in case one of them was injured.

9 – THE BLACK MARKET.

Before leaving, Alice explained to Walter that it was important that they remain discreet throughout the trip. They had to avoid being noticed, as it would attract the attention of the brigands. Alice also insisted that they should always stay together, as it was their best chance of survival.

Once they left their shelter, Alice and Walter walked for hours through the forest. Alice had planned regular stops to rest and eat, so that they would not be tired when they arrived in the city. They walked cautiously, avoiding no noise, and avoiding areas where bandits might be present.

Finally, after two days of walking, Alice and Walter reached the city of brigands. They stopped the main entrances to the city and instead looked for a more discreet place to enter. Alice used the false identities she had obtained to pass the city guards, who were suspicious of strangers.

Once in the city, Alice and Walter blended into the crowd, wearing their discreet clothes, and avoiding glances. They looked for the black-market stall where the item they were looking for was located. However, they soon realized that it would not be easy, as bandits were everywhere, and the streets were dangerous.

Alice and Walter walked through the dense crowd of the city of brigands, avoiding the curious eyes of the locals.

"Stay close to me, Walter. We have to be careful here. Hey" said, Alice.

"Okay. But how are we going to find the object we are looking for? The city is huge, and brigands are everywhere."

"We have to find the black market. This is where the brigands sell their illegal goods. If we can access it, we will have a chance to find what we are looking for."

"But how are we going to find the black market? We can't just ask someone where they are." Walter replied.

"I know. We need to find clues. We need to observe and listen carefully to see if we hear anything that could help us."

"Okay, I'll be careful."

Alice and Walter continued to sneak through the crowd, watching their surroundings.

Suddenly, Alice saw a man exchanging money with another man in a narrow alley.

"Walter, look over there. This man appears to be making illegal transactions. Maybe he can help us find the black market." Alice explains.

"How are we going to approach it? We cannot simply ask him where the black market is."

"I will try to approach it discreetly. You stay here and monitor our environment."

Alice approached the man and began to talk with him in whispers.

"Excuse me, sir. I'm new to this city and I need to find something. I wonder if you could help me." Alice asks in a small voice.

The man looked at Alice suspiciously.

"And what are you looking for?" Ask the young man.

"I'm looking for the black market. I have heard that this is the place where bandits sell their illegal goods."

The man smiled.

"The black market, huh? It is a dangerous place for foreigners. You shouldn't go."

"But I need to find something. I am willing to take the risk."

The man thought for a moment.

"Okay. I can help you find the black market. But it will cost you dearly."

Alice took out a small sum of Bryan's relic items from her pocket and handed it to the man.

"That's all I have. I hope that will be enough. Hey" said, Alice.

The man took the money and drove Alice and Walter through the narrow streets of the city of brigands to the black market. Alice and Walter were amazed by the variety of illegal goods on display.

Alice and Walter were now on the black market in the city of robbers. The market was located in an unsolicited area of the city, hidden behind abandoned buildings and dark alleys. The stalls were made of raw wood and the objects were displayed on the floor. The market consisted of small groups of people who spoke in low voices, exchanging items in bags and crates.

The market was crowded with children, each with a stack of toys for sale. The toys were mostly hand-carved wooden toys, rag dolls, wooden hoops, leather balls, and card games. Some children sold used toys, while others offered new toys that were still wrapped.

The children were all dressed in a simple and dirty way. Most of them were barefoot, clothes torn, hair dirty and tangled. They were all very suspicious of Alice and Walter, strangers, and intruders in their market.

The children also sold stolen items, tools, and other illicit goods. Some stalls were for food products, but it was clear that most of the food was stolen or obtained through illegal means. The stalls were dirty and dilapidated, with no signs of hygiene.

The vendors, on the other hand, were often children dressed more elegantly than other children, and appeared to be members of criminal gangs. They were armed with wooden batons, looked suspiciously at shoppers, and kept a close eye on children selling toys. Alice and Walter were clearly strangers, and they felt that the salesmen were watching them suspiciously.

Despite the dangerousness of the place, Alice and Walter could not abandon their mission. They had to find the object they were looking for and get out of the city as quickly as possible. So they mingled with the crowd, discreetly looking for the stall that sold their coveted object.

'It's unbelievable. I didn't know you could find so much here. Alice tells Walter.

"Look at this, Alice. This is the object we are looking for!"

Walter grabbed Alice's arms and discreetly guided her to a stall where a fifteen-year-old girl was selling various items. On the shelf was a small wooden box with a glass window that showed Bryan's watch. This box was locked by a small golden metal padlock, adding even more mystery to the precious object it contained.

Bryan's watch was a beautiful piece. It had a brown leather strap and a silver dial engraved with Roman numerals. The dial was slightly scratched, but Alice could see that the watch had been carefully maintained.

The fifteen-year-old girl who sold Bryan's watch was short and thin, with curly brown hair and bright green eyes. She wore a black lace dress, leather boots and had a defiant expression on her face. She looked much younger than the other street vendors, but Alice could feel the hardness in her eyes. This young girl had certainly had to go through difficult experiences to find herself selling illegal items on the black market.

"How can we get this locked box?" asked Alice to Walter.

'I will try to talk to the girl and see if she is willing to sell her. If that doesn't work, we'll have to find a way to steal it discreetly. But we have to be careful. Sellers don't take their eyes off us. Walter replied cautiously.

Walter approached the girl carefully and struck up a conversation. Alice could see that he was winning the price of the watch, but she couldn't hear what they were saying. She carefully observed the girl, trying to determine if she was trustworthy. The girl seemed suspicious and restless, but after a few minutes of negotiations, she finally handed the locked wooden box to Walter in exchange for a few silver coins.

Alice's heart was pounding as they walked out of the crowd with the box in their possession. They quickly roamed the streets, tried to leave the city before being discovered. Eventually, they reached the edge of town and stopped to catch their breath.

"We did it!" exclaimed Alice loosely. "We found Bryan's watch!"

"But we are not out of danger yet," Walter replied, wiping the sweat from his brow. "We need to make sure we are not being tracked. And we must be prepared for anything that might happen on our way home."

Alice looks at the wooden box worriedly. “I don’t have the key,” she told Walter. “And the girl didn’t give it to us either.”

Walter sighed. “We have to go back to the black market,” he says. “We have to find the key before we leave here.”

Alice nodded, but she was very nervous. Returning to the black market was already an ordeal but doing it with Bryan’s watch was even riskier. They began to march towards the city, staying out of sight as much as possible.

When they hit the black market, it was even more chaotic than the first time. The child vendors were even more aggressive, and the customers seemed even more suspicious. Alice and Walter searched for the girl who had sold them in the box, but she was nowhere to be found. Eventually, they found another vendor, a twelve-year-old boy who seemed to know a lot about the black market.

"I'm looking for the key to this box," Walter says, pointing to the child's wooden box.

The child smiled. "I can help you," he said. "But it's going to be expensive."

Walter took a handful of toy cars out of his bag and put them in the child's hand. "That's all I have," he says.

The child accepted the toy cars with a smirk and took out a small rusty key from his pocket. "That's your key", he said.

Alice took the key and tried it on the padlock. It took a little strength, but eventually, the padlock gave way. She opened the box and took out Bryan's watch. She sighed with sagging as she looked at it, feeling a little safer now that she was in possession of the watch again.

But as they turned around to leave, they noticed that they were surrounded by a group of vendors from around fifteen years, all armed with wooden batons and knives. "You can't live like this," said one, one of them who had dark skin.

Alice and Walter exchanged a look, knowing they were trapped. They were surrounded on all sides, with nowhere to go. They slowly pulled out their handguns, preparing to defend themselves.

Alice and Walter stood on alert, ready at any moment to retaliate for an impending attack. The vendors approached slowly, encircling the duo. Alice had a metal baton in her right hand, while Walter pulled a knife out of his belt. The vendors seemed suspicious and were ready to attack.

"What do you want?" asked Walter in a loud and clear voice.

"We want the watch," the gang leader replied with a sly smile.

"The watch belongs to us, and it is out of the question of you the data," says Alice pointing to the watch in her left hand. "We're not letting her go."

"Then you're going to die for her," replied the chief, nodding to his men to attack.

Alice and Walter threw themselves into the fray, using their weapons to defend themselves against the vendors. The situation was dangerous and chaotic, with stab and baton blows exchanged on both sides. Alice managed to hit two of the robbers with his metal baton, while Walter managed to stab another. But the number of sellers was higher, and the two heroes were soon overwhelmed.

That's when a familiar voice holds in the air. "Stop!"

Alice and Walter turned to see their friend, Jake, the boyfriend of Alice's sister, Mathilda, appears with a group of city guards. The salesmen, seeing that they were outnumbered, began to slowly retreat, before running away. Alice, Walter, and Jake kissed, happy to finally meet again. City guards escorted them out of the danger zone, protecting them from vendors and other city dangers from brigands.

Once safe, Jake explained that he had seen Elliot and that Elliot was worried because he knew that Alice and Walter would come to the city of the Brigands. Elliot had enlisted Jake's help to ensure that Alice and Walter were not in danger. Jake had alerted the city guards for help rescuing his friend Walter. He then asked to help them to people who serve as informants for the Directorate of Internal Security to find them, which led them to them. Alice, Walter, and Jake then set out on the journey home, safe this time, Bryan's watch safe and sound with them.

After being escorted out of the Brigands' town, Alice, Walter, and Jake stopped to rest. Alice turned to Jake and asked him for a comment he knew she was looking for Bryan's watch. Jake looked down, looking uncomfortable.

"Listen, Alice, I'm sorry, but I work for the Directorate of Internal Security. Elliot contacted me because he was worried about you and Walter, and I'm in charge of monitoring everything that's going on in the Brigands' City. So I followed your movements and discovered that you were looking for Bryan's watch. But I couldn't leave you in danger, so I contacted the city guards to help you. "

Alice stared at Jake, trying to figure out how she felt. She felt both betrayed and grateful. She was betrayed, on the one hand, because Elliot had kept it secret and, on the other hand, because she thought she was being watched as if she were an enemy of their peoples. But she was great because he had looked out for her safety.

"I'm glad you came to our rescue, Jake," she said at last. "But I knew that looking for Bryan's watch could put me in danger, especially with Yann and the Grand Council looking for me.

You should know that I am willing to take risks to help my family and friends."

Jake nodded, seeming to understand the logic. "I know, Alice. That's an admirable quality, but you also need to know when you're putting your life at risk. I'm glad you're safe now."

Alice smiled faintly, knowing that Jake was right. She was happy to be safe with Walter and Bryan's watch, but she knew it was just beginning.

"How is my younger sister Mathilda?" she asked Jake, offering to change the subject.

Jake smiled slightly. "She's fine thanked you for her. She was worried about you too, but I told her you were safe with Walter."

Alice nodded, sensing a hint of jealousy at the thought that her younger sister Mathilda had someone to protect her. She shook her head, tried to chase away that thought.

"That's good," she said simply. "You know, Jake, you're more than a friend to me. You are a member of my family now. And I want you to know that I'll always be there for you, no matter what happens."

Jake smiled and seemed touched by the words Alice had just spoken and then he said. "I know, Alice. And I, too, will always be there for you and Walter."

They smiled at each other, knowing that their friendship had been strengthened by the events they had been through. They continued their journey home, ready to face what lay ahead.

Alice, Jake, and Walter finally arrived at Alice's house, relieved to finally be safe. To their surprise, Elliot was already waiting for them, eager to see them safe and sound. The four of them kissed, happy to be together again.

Elliot then asked how their trip to the city of the Brigands went, and Alice began to recount their adventure, starting with their meeting with the vendors until they fled with the help of Jake and the city guards. She also explained how they finally found Bryan's watch and how they brought it back to them.

It was then that Alice noticed that Yann, a member of the Grand Council, had arrived at her house. She wondered if it was a coincidence or if he had come for Bryan's watch. She exchanged a worried look with Elliot, who seemed to share her thoughts.

Yann greeted everyone in the room, then asked Alice if she had any news of Bryan's watch that had been missing for several years. Alice nodded nodding and told him they hadn't found it and that she would look for a new lead about the watch elsewhere. Yann seemed troubled and Alice noticed a hint of suspicion in his eyes.

Elliot then decided to break the ice by inviting Yann to join them for dinner. Yann agreed, but Alice could sense a palpable tension in the room. She tried to stay calm, but she was worried about what it meant for the future.

During dinner, they talked about everything and nothing, but Alice could sense that something was wrong. She wondered if Yann had any doubts about their trip to the city of the Brigands or if he was looking for something in particular. She exchanged a worried look with Elliot, who also seemed to be wondering.

Once dinner was over, Yann took his leave, but before leaving, he gave Alice a strong look. She could feel his eyes on her as he left the house, and she shuddered as she wondered what was going to happen next.

Once Yann was gone, Alice, Elliot, Jake, and Walter found themselves in the living room. Alice was worried and she could feel that others were too.

Elliot broke the silence by asking, "What do you think? Does Yann know the truth about Bryan's watch?"

Jake quickly replied, "I don't know. But this possibility cannot be ruled out. He is dangerous and I am sure he does not mean us all good."

Walter added, "I agree with Jake. Yann is a criminal and I don't trust him."

Alice nodded, sharing the same feelings as the others. She thought for a while before saying, "We have to be careful. It is clear that he is looking for something and we cannot afford to underestimate his dangerousness."

Elliot added, "I agree. We must be vigilant and ready to act if necessary. We cannot afford to take risks."

Alice sighed, feeling the pressure mount. She already had a lot of problems to deal with and Yann's arrival had only added to her stress. She tried to focus on the current situation and find a solution.

She looked at others and said, "We need to work together to find a solution. We need to find a way to find out what Yann is looking for and protect ourselves."

The others nodded in approval. They knew the situation was serious and that they had to act quickly to protect themselves.

The tension was palpable in the room as they began discussing next steps. They all knew that Yann's threat was real and that they had to be ready for anything that could happen.

Alice spoke again, supposedly hearing that she had an idea: "Maybe we can try to hide Bryan's watch somewhere where he can't find it. We can put it in a safe place, where he won't be able to discover it. This might give us some time to think about our next step."

Elliot pondered Alice's suggestion. "It's a good idea, but where can we hide it? We can't just leave it at home or in a place known to everyone."

Jake suggested, "Maybe we can hide it in a safe deposit box at the bank? It is a safe place, and we can access it easily if we need to."

Walter added, "Or we can entrust it to a trusted friend, someone who can keep it for us and return it when we need it."

Alice agreed, recognizing the validity of both suggestions. "I think these are good options, but we have to choose the safest one. We cannot afford to take risks."

Elliot added: "We also need to make sure Yann doesn't follow us. We must be careful not to give clues as to where we are going to hide the watch."

The tension was palpable in the room as they began to hatch a plan to hide Bryan's watch. They knew it wouldn't solve all their problems, but it was a start. They had to work together and be ready to act quickly if necessary.

Alice concluded the discussion by saying, "We need to act quickly and be prepared for anything that might happen. We cannot afford to underestimate Yann. We have to be ready for anything."

10 – THE LAST HOPE.

After discussing options to hide Bryan's watch from Yann, Alice, Elliot, Jake, and Walter decided to put it back in the box and hide it. But before they did, they had to make sure Yann couldn't find the key to the box. So they decided to place the key in a small box and drop it off at Alice's sister's house.

The small box was made of wood and was shaped like a heart. It was covered with delicate pink paper and had a small ribbon attached to the lock. Inside the box was a small red velvet cushion that contained the key to the box. The cushion was held in place by a white satin ribbon.

After placing the key in the box, they

decided to hide it in a safe place at Alice's sister's house. They chose an unobvious place to prevent Yann from finding her, even if he was visiting the house. They finally opted for the bottom of a drawer of the chest of drawers in the guest room. It was a safe place and unlikely to be discovered.

Once they placed the small box in the dresser drawer, they took a deep breath and looked at each other, relieved. They knew it was far from a perfect solution, but it gave them some time to find a more permanent solution. They decided to continue working together and remain vigilant against Yann's threat.

After hiding Bryan's watch key at Alice's sister's house, the four friends began to feel a little safer, but they knew their work wasn't done. They knew that Yann would not let go easily and that they had to find a more permanent solution to hide the watch.

They decided to put in place some additional security measures. They decided to set up guard towers in Mathilda's house and in Alice's house, to monitor Yann's comings and goings. They have also set up a code to alert the police in case of intrusion by Yann or one of his accomplices.

But they didn't stop there. They also began to develop a safety plan for themselves, knowing that Yann could be dangerous and unpredictable. They agreed not to go to places alone. They also planned to meet regularly to discuss the situation and their security plan. They also chose not to keep the watch in one place permanently, but to move it regularly between several safe places.

With their security organization in place, they felt much safer. They followed their personal safety plan and continued to meet regularly to discuss the situation.

After taking extra security measures to protect Bryan's watch, the four friends began investigating Yann to find out why he was so determined to get his hands on the watch. They began searching Yann's file at the Directorate of Internal Security to find information to learn more about him.

They soon discovered that Yann was in trouble with a young thug from the city of robbers and that he had been involved in several theft cases in the past, but that one person had sought to suppress the evidence. It made them realize that Bryan's watch might not be the only thing he wanted. So they started looking for other valuable possessions that might interest Yann.

They also started monitoring Yann's movements and noticed that he was watching Alice's house. So they decided to follow him to see if he had accomplices or if he was preparing something suspicious. After a few days of surveillance, they discovered that Yann did indeed have accomplices and that he was preparing a burglary.

Jake and Walter were sitting in Alice's living room, discussing the awkward situation they were engaged in. They knew that Yann and his accomplices were determined to steal Bryan's watch, which was currently stored at the home of Alice's sister Mathilda.

"I'm worried about Mathilda's safety," says Jake, "We need to find a way to protect her."

Walter agreed, "I agree, but how can we do that? We can't just monitor it for twenty-four hours a day. We need to find a way to protect the watch without putting anyone at risk."

"I think we have to watch the clock ourselves," Jake offered. "We can take turns to keep her safe until Yann abandons his plan. We cannot let Mathilda be hurt or the watch stolen."

Walter thought for a moment before answering, "That's a good idea, but we have to be careful. We all know that Yann is dangerous. We cannot take risks."

Jake nodded, "I know, but I'd rather watch the watch ourselves than risk something happening to Mathilda."

Walter smiled slightly, "You're right. We need to monitor the watch together. We must be vigilant and ensure that nothing happens."

Jake also smiled, "I'm glad you agree. We must remain united to protect the watch."

The two friends shook hands and began to set up their plan to monitor the watch. They knew it would be a difficult task, but they were determined to protect their friend and his precious object.

Despite their determination, they can't help but feel anxiety and fear. They knew Yann was dangerous and risked their lives watching the clock. But they also knew they had to do everything they could to protect Mathilda's house, Mathilda herself, and Bryan's precious watch, no matter the cost.

Jake and Walter had been taking turns monitoring Mathilda's house for a few days already. They felt stressed and nervous, knowing that Yann and his accomplices could attack at any moment. But they remained determined to protect Bryan's watch and Mathilda's house.

One evening, around twenty-two forty-five, Walter was drinking hot chocolate with marshmallows when he felt a violent blow to the back of the head. He collapses on the ground, sounded, and disoriented. Everything has become blurry around him, and he loses consciousness.

A few hours later, Jake arrived to take over from Walter. He was shocked to find his friend lifeless on the ground. He knelt down next to him and checked his pulse. Fortunately, Walter was still breathing, but it was obvious that he had been attacked.

Jake immediately calls Alice and Elliot. Afterwards, he tries to wake up his friend. Finally, after a few seemingly endless moments, Walter opened his eyes and looked around, still disoriented.

"What happened?" he asked in a weak voice.

"You got hit in the back of the head," Jake replied, helping his friend Walter to sit up. "Help will arrive soon."

Walter blinked, trying to gather his memories. "I don't remember anything," he said, touching his bruised head.

Jake reassured him, "Don't worry, everything is fine now. We will stay here until the others arrive and we will continue to monitor the house together."

Walter nodded, still a little stunned, but grateful to be alive. He realized then that their surveillance mission was more dangerous than he had imagined and that they had to be even more careful. Even so, he felt determined to protect the watch and stop Yann and his accomplices before they hurt anyone else.

Walter frantically rummaged through his pockets, desperately searching for something. Jake, intrigued, asked him what he was looking for.

"The keys to the little box and the box where we hid Bryan's watch," Walter replies anxiously. "I hid them in one of my pockets to protect them, but now they are gone."

Jake looks at his friend worriedly. "Are you sure you put them in your pockets?" he said. "Maybe you left them somewhere?"

Walter shook his head, "No, I'm sure I put them in my pockets. I felt them when I sat down to drink my hot chocolate. But now they are gone."

Walter felt overcome with guilt and anger. He had been tasked with protecting the watch, but he had failed. Now the watch was in great danger, and he didn't know how to retrieve it without the keys.

Jake realized that this meant that someone had entered the house and stolen the keys while Walter was unconscious. He knew it put Bryan's watch at risk.

"We need to find those keys," Jake said as he stood up. "Otherwise, Yann and his accomplices could easily steal the watch."

Walter nodded, "I know. But how are we going to find them? We need these keys to protect the watch."

Jake thought for a moment before

answering, "We have to search the house. Maybe the thieves dropped them somewhere while fleeing."

Walter nodded, "Okay. We will look at every corner of the house. We cannot afford to leave this watch in the wrong hands."

The two friends began to search the house, examining every room, every drawer, every piece of furniture. They frantically searched for the keys to the small box and box where Bryan's watch was stored.

Unfortunately, after several hours of intensive searching, they found no trace of the keys. Jake and Walter looked at each other, discouraged and frustrated. They knew this meant that the watch was now in great danger.

Jake took a deep breath, "We have to keep looking. Maybe we missed something."

Walter agreed, "Yes, we have to be methodical. We cannot give up."

The two friends continued to search, determined to find the missing keys. They knew Mathilda's life and the safety of the watch were at stake.

Suddenly, voices were heard outside the house. Jake and Walter exchanged a look of great dismay. Alice, Elliot, and Mathilda eventually arrived. Jake greets them and quickly brings them inside. He explains the situation to their three friends, their comment about Walter had been attacked from behind and how the keys had disappeared.

Mathilda was upset. The watch was a valuable asset that belonged to Bryan, and it had been designated in his custody. She couldn't imagine that someone could steal it. Elliot, meanwhile, immediately set to work, inspecting the house for any evidence or clues that might help them find the missing keys. Alice, for her part, offers to contact members of the Internal Security to report the theft and asks for help to find the culprits.

Meanwhile, Jake and Walter continued to search the house, desperately looking for clues or leads. But despite their best efforts, they found nothing useful.

The tension rose as the hours passed. They knew that every minute that passed increased the risk of the watch being stolen or damaged. Eventually, Elliot found a crumpled piece of paper under the couch. He unfolded it and handed it to Jake. It was a handwritten note, with detailed instructions on how to get the watch. Jake read the note aloud for everyone to hear.

"If you want to collect the keys, you must bring the watch to the place indicated on this card. If you contact the authorities or try to play the heroes, you will never see the keys again, and we will hunt you down to the end of the world. You have 24 hours to bring us the keys. Don't disappoint us."

Mathilda's friends were shocked. They knew it was an exorbitant and dangerous demand, but they couldn't afford to lose the watch. They looked at each other, knowing that they had to act quickly and carefully.

The group was now in shock. They were all worried about the safety of the watch, but also about their own safety. No one knew who was responsible for the note or why they wanted the watch and keys. Mathilda's friends knew they had to act quickly, but they were also aware of the danger of this situation.

Jake spoke: "We have to organize to get the keys and the watch, but we have to do it carefully. We don't know who we're dealing with, and we don't want to endanger anyone's life. Everyone nodded, knowing that Jake was right.

Elliot had a plan. He knew where the location on the map was. It was an abandoned area on the outskirts of the city, away from prying eyes. He knew it was dangerous, but he was willing to take the risk. The other members of the group nodded, knowing they had no other choice.

The group set off, heading towards the location shown on the map. They were all very nervous, knowing that they might be being followed or monitored. The journey was made in tense silence, each immersed in his own thoughts. Eventually, they arrived at their destination.

The place was desolate and abandoned, as Elliot had described. Elliot took the watch out of his backpack and put it on the floor. He waits patiently for someone to pick them up.

After a few minutes, a sound of footsteps was heard. A young man appeared to be a trade-for-trade correspondent to the leader of the group of brigands who had surrounded Alice and Walter at the black-market level in the city of brigands. The latter came out of the shadows. He walked towards the group and stopped in front of the clock. He inspected it thoroughly before turning back to the group.

"The keys are inside this box", he said in a low but threatening voice. "You can get the box now."

Jake stepped forward cautiously and took the box the man was handing him. The keys were inside, as promised. Jake thanked the man before slowly backing away, joining the other members of the group.

Once they were safe, Jake opened the box to retrieve the keys. He carefully checked that it was their keys, relieved to find that it was still in good condition. Mathilda's friends sighed to reduce knowing that the keys were now safe.

The return home was silent, each one immersed in his own thoughts. They knew that this situation was not yet resolved. Mathilda's friends knew they had to remain vigilant and keep looking for answers. But for now, they were relieved that the keys were safe and sound.

Once back at Mathilda's house, the group was relieved to be safe. Jake, who used to take the lead, explained to the other members of the small group what he noticed during the exchange: Yann's presence. Jake didn't know if Yann was involved in the attack on Walter, but he felt he was more than just an observer. Alice, Mathilda's sister, even suspected Yann of being the accomplice of the brigands. If this was the case, then Yann was even more dangerous than they had imagined.

The group then began to discuss how they would get the watch back. They now had all the keys, but they knew that the robbers were still looking for them. They therefore had to act quickly and effectively. Jake suggested that they wait until night and return to the place of exchange. He also offered to bring weapons to protect himself, but the other members of the group disagreed.

Mathilda, the owner of the house where the watch was hidden, felt responsible for the situation. She didn't want her friends to put their lives on the line for her. She therefore suggested contacting the Internal Security Service and giving them the keys. Jake explains, "Princess, I don't agree with you."

"And why is that?" asks Mathilda.

Jake replies, "Simply because we don't know if Yann doesn't have accomplices in the Internal Security Service."

Alice said, "Sorry Mathilda, but now I'm right with Jake."

The group was now divided on how best to act. Jake and Alice were convinced that the best option was to return to the place of exchange and retrieve the watch, while Mathilda and Elliot thought it would be safer to contact Homeland Security.

Eventually, Jake convinced the group that their only chance of getting the watch back was to get it herself. He explained to them that they had to be quick and efficient, because the brigands could be on their trail. However, it was also important not to put their lives in danger unnecessarily, which is why he suggested not carry weapons.

Jake's plan was to go to the exchange site at night when the robbers would probably be less vigilant. They could act quickly, retrieve the watch, and leave before the robbers spotted them. The members of the small group accepted Jake's plan, but with some trepidation.

They prepared for their mission and set off for the place of exchange. Along the way, Jake explained to Mathilda and Alice the different steps of their plan. Once there, they hid behind the bushes and waited patiently.

After a few minutes, the brigands appear. They were apparently looking for something or someone and hadn't noticed the group's presence. Jake was right, the night was their ally. The group watched the bandits from afar, until they found what they were looking for and headed for their respective bikes.

That's when the group decided to act. They came out of hiding and ran towards the brigands. The brigands, caught off guard, could do nothing to defend themselves. The group retrieved the watch and quickly walked away.

They returned to Mathilda's house, relieved to have accomplished their mission. They looked at the watch with admiration, realizing that it had great historical value. Mathilda, moved, thanked the group for their precious help.

The band celebrated their success with hot chocolate and pastries. They were aware that they had taken a risk by recovering the watch, but they were proud to have managed to recover it without violence.

The group had successfully accomplished their mission, but they knew their adventure was not over. They were still in danger, and it was possible that the brigands would seek revenge.

They had to remain vigilant and ready to act when needed.

After describing their success, Alice, Mathilda, and Jake turned to Walter, who looked a little lost. Alice approached him and asked, “Do you know why these keys and this watch are so important to us, but also to you?”

Walter shook his head, looking at Alice curiously. Alice then explains: “These keys and this watch are linked to your return home. They open the doors that allow you to go home, and the watch shows the precise moment when this needs to be done.”

Walter seems puzzled. “How can you know that?” he asks.

Alice smiled. “It’s a long story, but we met someone who explained the meaning of these objects. If you trust us, we can help you get home.”

Walter thought for a moment, then nodded. “Okay, I trust you. But what are the conditions for me to return home?”

Mathilda spoke: “The doors will only open for a specific hour, and we will have to be there to accompany you. In addition, there is a spell that prevents anyone from leaving this place without permission. We have a plan to get around it, but we have to be very careful."

Walter seems a little worried. "What if something goes wrong? What happens if we don't succeed?"

Jake interjected: "We have a solid plan, and we managed to get the watch back without violence. We will be ready to act when needed, but it is important that you have confidence in us."

Walter nodded. "I trust you," he said in a firm voice.

Mathilda smiled. "So it's decided. We will prepare for the moment when the doors open. We can't miss this chance to take you home."

The group then began planning the steps of their next mission, determined to help Walter return home. They knew the stakes were high, but they were willing to risk anything to help their new friend.

Alice, Mathilda, and Jake gather around a table to discuss the plan to get to the 'Gates of the Journey of No Return'. They knew it was a dangerous place and they had to be ready for anything.

Alice spoke first: "First, we must go to the 'Hill of Four Winds' west of here. This is where the doors we are looking for are."

Mathilda continued: "Then we will have to face the 'Hartians'. They are formidable, but we have learned a spell that will allow us to pass them safely."

Jake added: "Once we have passed through the 'Hartians', we will have to place Bryan's watch on a blue crystal base. This will activate the doors."

Alice continued, "Finally, we will have to use the keys. First, we will have to put the green key in the red lock, and then the red key in the blue lock. It is important not to put the keys in one of the other five locks, otherwise it will activate an alarm."

Mathilda asked a question: "And what about security around the doors? We know that this place is very well protected."

Jake replied, "We've planned that as well. We have developed a plan to avoid the guards and deflect the traps. But we will have to be very careful."

Alice finds, "This is our plan. We have worked hard to put it in place, but we know there are risks. We have to be ready for anything."

Mathilda adds: "I agree. We must be ready to face whatever comes our way. We are a strong and united team, and we will succeed together."

The group then began to discuss the details of the plan, preparing for their mission. They knew it wouldn't be easy, but they were willing to do anything to help Walter get home.

Alice, Mathilda, Elliot, Jake, and Walter had gathered in the common room of their headquarters to prepare for their journey to the "Gates of the Journey of No Return." Each of them had taken weapons: knives, batons, shields and helmets to protect themselves in case of attack. They had also prepared food for their trip, knowing they wouldn't be able to rely on restaurants on their way. They had provisions for several days, as well as sleeping bags and tents to rest.

Elliot looked nervous and worried. "I'm not sure it's a good idea," he says. "We don't know what awaits us there. What if something goes wrong?"

Alice calmly replied, "Don't worry Elliot, we have a solid plan in place. We have everything planned and we are ready to deal with any situation. We are a strong and united team, and we will succeed together."

Jake adds, "That's right, we've worked hard to prepare for this mission. We know it won't be easy, but we're willing to do anything to help Walter get home."

Walter looked at his friends, appreciating their support, but worry crept into his mind. "I don't want you to risk your life for me," he said, his voice betraying his anxiety.

Mathilda put her hand on Walter's shoulder. "We're here for you, Walter. We know you would do the same for us if we were in the same situation. We will take you home, safely."

Elliot, with tears in his eyes, said, "I'm sorry. I should have been braver. It's just that I'm worried about all of us."

Alice smiled softly. "Don't worry, Elliot, we all have moments of doubt and uncertainty.

But we're there for each other, and that's what makes us stronger together."

The group began to work diligently to complete preparations for their trip. Preparations for the trip were now in full swing. Alice had gathered everything needed for the trip, including backpacks for everyone, food and water for several days, and a detailed map of the area. The weapons were also ready, each of the members of the group had a knife, a baton, a shield, and a helmet.

Jake, meanwhile, was busy checking the map and studying the plans. He wanted to make sure the group was ready for any protection. Mathilda, on the other hand, dedicates herself to preparing food for the trip. She had provided energy bars, dried fruit, and bottled water, and had organized everything carefully.

But despite all the careful preparations, Elliot still seemed worried as Walter. Alice notices Walter's worried expression and approaches him. "Walter are you okay?" she asks softly.

Walter shook his head. "I don't know, Alice. It all seems so dangerous. What if something happened to one of us?"

Alice put her hand on Walter's shoulder. "We're all together, Walter. We will protect each other, no matter what."

Alice's words seemed to reassure Walter, who smiled shyly. "Okay, I trust the team," he says.

The group finally finished the preparations and set off for the Gates of the Journey of No Return. They knew there would be dangers in their path, but they were aware of their preparation and collective strength.

11 – RETURN HOME.

The group of Alice, Mathilda, Elliot, Jake, and Walter had embarked on a risky adventure by going to the Gates of the Journey of No Return. Their journey had begun on a steep path, surrounded by steep cliffs and majestic mountains. The wind was blowing hard, slamming the tents and backpacks of the travelers. Despite this, the group was moving fast, determined to reach their destination.

They had walked for hours without meeting a living soul. The only sounds that accompanied them were the sound of their footsteps and the blowing wind. Suddenly, they hear a terrifying roar that startles them. They drew their weapons, ready to defend themselves against any threat. However, there was nothing on the horizon, except a vast expanse of sand and rocks.

Suddenly, a shape appeared in the distance. It was a strange animal, with glowing fur and sparkling eyes. He looked menacing but didn't seem aggressive. The group decided to continue on their way, remaining on guard.

Later that day, they arrived at a tumultuous river blocking their path. They looked for a way to cross, but there was no bridge in sight. Eventually, they decided to build a raft with branches and rope, so they could cross the river. After several hours of hard work, the raft was ready, and the group managed to cross the river safely.

They continued their journey through desert plains, where the winds blew strongly, and temperatures could be extreme. They had a detailed map of the area, which allowed them to follow their route and orient themselves without difficulty.

Along the way, they came across other strange animals, such as birds with blade-shaped wings and two-headed snakes. The group was fascinated by these creatures, but remained vigilant, as they did not know what to expect.

The group of Alice, Mathilda, Elliot, Jake, and Walter had traveled a long distance since their departure to the 'Gates of the Journey of No Return'. They were exhausted and their food and water supplies were starting to run out. However, their concern grew as they realized they were being followed by an unknown group.

Jake was the first to notice furtive movements in the shadow of the mountains that stood on the horizon. He had an unpleasant intuition that this group was not friends with them. He turns to the other members of the group to share his concerns. Alice, Mathilda, Elliot, and

Walter looked at everything in the direction it pointed and also saw the suspicious movements.

The group decided to continue walking, but at a faster pace and keeping a watchful eye on their surroundings. They feared an ambush and made the decision to divide up the available weapons, in order to be ready in case of attack. Jake considers his bow, while Mathilda had her dagger in her hand. Elliot had his battle axe ready, Alice his spear and Walter his whip.

The group continued to move forward, but the tension was palpable. They didn't talk much anymore except to exchange discreet signals to communicate their concern. They were getting closer and closer to the mountain, where the group following them had established their hiding place.

Suddenly, an arrow whistled through the air, narrowly missing Elliot's head. The group immediately moved into combat position and responded to the attack by launching a volley of arrows at their attackers. They could momentarily see the face of Yann and that of the leader of the brigands they had met before their departure before their enemy hid again behind the rocks.

The battle raged, with brigands coming out of hiding to attack the group, but also with bladed birds and two-headed snakes that seemed to belong to the brigands, preying on the travelers. The fight was fierce, but the group of Alice, Mathilda, Elliot, Jake, and Walter, thanks to their skill and determination, managed to repel the robbers and get to safety.

The group was exhausted and injured, but they were relieved that they had managed to defeat the robbers and to be able to continue their journey to "the Gates of the Journey of No Return". They had learned an important lesson: never let your guard down, even in an environment as strange and mysterious as this. They set out again, knowing that other dangers awaited them on their way, but with the certainty that their determination would enable them to overcome all obstacles.

They finally reach their destination, The Gates of the Journey of No Return. It was a huge stone arch, carved into the rock, which seemed to lead to another world. Behind the stone arch, one could glimpse a huge golden door. Alice explains that according to what she could read about this place, the door would weigh about fifteen kilograms and that it was made of gold of twenty-four karats. The group approached cautiously, aware of the possible dangers that awaited them on the other side of the stone arch. They stood ready to deal with any situation.

Suddenly, out of nowhere, two Hartians appeared. The Hartians are a breed of large four-headed wolf. Their job is to guard the door. The Hartians were imposing, their fur was intensely black, and their four heads seemed to scrutinize every movement of the group. The travelers stood still, looking at each other with some concern. They knew they had to stay calm and not panic, but it was hard not to be intimidated by these imposing creatures.

Alice spoke in a clear and confident voice, trying to communicate with the Hartians in the hope of finding a peaceful solution to their meeting. But the Hartians did not seem to be interested in any communication. They growled and showed their sharp fangs, pushing the group back slightly.

Mathilda looked at the Hartians with an expression of fear mixed with fascination. She was fascinated by the power and beauty of these creatures, but she knew that they could be extremely dangerous if they decided to attack them.

Elliot was on alert, ready to act when needed. He looked calm, but his muscles were tense, ready to react to the slightest threat. He kept an eye on the Hartians while monitoring the surroundings for other possible dangers.

Jake was nervous, he had his eyes fixed on the Hartians, not knowing how to react. He had heard about the reputation of the Hartians, and he knew that their meeting was a critical moment that could determine their fate.

Walter, meanwhile, remained stoic, observing the Hartians with an imperturbable expression. He seemed to be thinking about how best to handle the situation.

After a few moments, Alice remembers that she must use the spell to get the Hartians to let the group of Alice, Mathilda, Elliot, Jake, and Walter passes.

Alice took a deep breath and closed her eyes for a few seconds to concentrate. Then she opened her eyes and began to incantate spell in Latin: "Hartiani, who transits, no praetermittite. Alas, prohibits." *(Hartians, who pass, let us pass. Prevent others.)* Her voice echoed clearly in the air as she cast the spell with conviction.

The Hartians seemed to be momentarily disoriented by the spell, shaking their heads, and growling. But they eventually calmed down and began to retreat, then decided to let the group pass. Alice had managed to use magic to command the Hartians to let them pass and prevent any other group from following.

Mathilda, Elliot, Jake, and Walter followed Alice as she walked with a brisk step towards the golden door. They passed the Hartians without incident, but they could feel their gaze fixed and menacing on them.

Once they had covered some distance, Mathilda turned to Alice and thanked her for allowing them to pass safely. Elliot followed suit and added that he was impressed by his spell. Jake confessed that he had been very scared and was relieved to be able to move forward.

Walter remained silent, but he looked relieved too. They had managed to pass safely thanks to Alice's skill in magic. They continued on their way towards the front door, knowing that their adventure had only just begun.

The group was making great strides, leaving the Hartians behind. They had managed to pass thanks to Alice's spell, but the experience had left them all a little shaken. They knew that they were far from out of danger and that each new stage of their journey could be even more difficult.

As they approached the great gold door, their attention was drawn to the brilliant brilliance of the golden surface. The gate was massive, measuring about 10 meters high and 5 meters wide. It was adorned with intricate patterns and symbols that seemed to have been engraved with great precision. The warm and golden colors of the door were reflected on the floor, creating an almost magical atmosphere.

The group stopped in front of the door, amazed by its beauty. Mathilda approached the door and gently touched it with her fingers, admiring the smooth, cold texture of the surface. Elliot and Jake stood next to her, staring at the door with an expression of respect.

Walter stood back, staring at the door with a scrutinizing look. He seemed to be thinking about the best way to open it, but he kept his thoughts to himself.

Alice watched the door with a mixture of curiosity and apprehension. She knew that the door could hide many dangers and that she had to be on her guard. She turned to the group and said, "We have arrived at the golden door. Now we have to find a way to open it. Let us remain vigilant and ready to act."

The group prepared to look for a way to open the door, but for now, they were all amazed by her beauty and majesty. They knew that their adventure was far from over, but for now, they were happy to have managed to get through the Hartians and arrive at the Golden Gate.

Alice searched around the gold door to find the blue crystal base. She searched the nooks and crannies, inspecting every stone and engraving. Finally, she saw the plinth hidden in the shadows, hidden behind a massive pillar. She approached carefully, fearing that something would appear out of nowhere and surprise her.

The blue crystal plinth was beautiful, with a light blue and translucent hue. It was cut with great precision, with smooth and sharp edges. Alice knew that the stand was very important to their mission, as it was the place where they had to place Bryan's watch to activate the portal. She took the pedestal carefully, making sure not to break it, and brought it back to the group.

Jake took Bryan's watch and gently placed it on the blue crystal base. He stepped back and watched in wonder as the plinth lit up with a bright blue glow. The light spread throughout the room, illuminating every nook and cranny and crack. The ground shook slightly, and the walls began to emit a strange and supernatural sound.

Mathilda moved closer to Jake and took his hand, squeezing hard for reassurance. Elliot took a step forward and put his hand on Alice's shoulder. Walter stood back, but he kept his eyes fixed on the gate opening in front of them.

The portal opened in a flash of blinding light, revealing a dark and mysterious passage. The group watched with trepidation, knowing that their adventure would now take an even more dangerous turn. Alice took a deep breath and said, "It's now or never. Let's go. The group walked through the portal in an instant, disappearing into the darkness of the unknown.

The group advanced into the dark corridor, darkness enveloping them on all sides. The ground under their feet was rough and uneven, as if they were walking on uneven stones. The walls were damp and cold, with traces of mold that suggested no one had been there for a long time. The only source of light was the blue glow that emanated from Bryan's watch, but it was insufficient to illuminate the entire hallway.

The group had barely walked a hundred meters when they began to hear frightening noises. There were muffled moans, hoarse grunts, and ominous rattling that seemed to come from all directions. The members of the group tensed, some clenched their fists, others tightened their grip on their weapons.

They finally came to a solid oak door that seemed to be the end of the corridor. The door was high and wide, with intricate decorations carved on the surface. Alice moved closer and examined the door more closely. She noticed five locks of different colors, blue, green, red, white, and purple, each of them had a hole of identical shape.

They began to think, trying to find a solution. Suddenly, Walter burst out laughing, "Well, we tried all the other doors using brute force, why not try using our brains this time?"

The group smiled, recognizing the wisdom of Walter's words. They began to think aloud, sharing their ideas and evaluating them together. They realized that each color was associated with one element: blue for water, green for earth, red for fire, white for air, and purple for spirit.

Jake took out of his bag the two keys; one green and one red. Alice reminded them that they had to put the green key in the red lock and the red key in the blue lock. She made a quick diagram to show her friends the correct combination.

Alice: "Jake, put the green key in the red lock and the red key in the blue lock, like this." She said, pointing to the diagram.

But just as Jake was about to insert the keys into the locks, Elliot took the keys from Jake's hands, looking at them with satisfaction. Everyone froze, shocked by this sudden action.

Elliot: "I'm sorry guys, but I'm here to stop you. I work for Yann, and my mission is to prevent Alice from taking over the presidency of the Grand Council of Children. You're all involved, so I'll have to take you with me."

The group was stunned, trying to understand the situation. Alice stepped forward, her face hard and determined.

Alice walked towards Elliot with a firm step, to clarify the situation. "Listen to me, Elliot, I have no intention of taking over the presidency of the Great Council of Children. I'm here to help my friend Walter get home. You have been manipulated by Yann, who is trying to take power over the Council. We are all innocent in this matter."

Jake nodded and spoke in turn. "Elliot, you don't understand what you're doing. Yann is not your friend. He just seeks to use others for his own interests. You have been deceived."

Mathilda joins the conversation by explaining in more detail the purpose of their expedition. "Our mission is to get Walter home. This door is the only way for him to get there. We don't want any trouble with you, Elliot. We are just innocent children trying to help a friend in need."

Elliot took a moment to think about what his classmates had just told him. He realized that Yann had deceived him and that he had made a mistake by taking the keys from them. He turns to Jake and returns the keys, his hands trembling. "I'm sorry guys, I was blinded by my personal ambitions. Yann manipulated me into arresting you. I regret what I did."

The group sighed in slack when they saw Elliot change their minds. They watched him leave, head down, knowing that he had become aware of his mistakes. They approached the door, inserted the keys into the right locks, and the door slowly opened.

Walter watches the sparkling white glow come out of the door opening, then turns to his friends with a sad, but grateful smile.

"Thank you all for coming with me." He says, looking at Alice, Jake, and Mathilda in turn. "I could never forget what you did for me today."

Alice approached him and took him in her arms, her eyes shining with tears. "We're glad we helped you, Walter. You are a dear friend to us all."

Jake nodded, a glimmer of sadness in his eyes. "We will miss you, Walter. We had a great time together."

Mathilda wiped a tear from her cheek and smiled sadly. "You're a true hero, Walter. I can never forget what you did for me."

Walter smiled, his eyes shining with gratitude and emotion. "I could never give you enough gratitude for your help, my friends. You've been amazing."

The group stood there for a moment, in silence, watching Walter slowly walk away towards the gleaming white glow. Then he turned around and waved goodbye. "Goodbye, my friends, maybe we'll meet again one day," he said before disappearing completely into the white light.

The group stands there for a while, still reeling from what they give to live, then turns to the now empty door. They knew they had accomplished something great and would never forget it.

Mary Jones sat next to her son's bed, her eyes on him. She noticed that his eyelids were moving slightly, as if he was trying to open them. She leaned towards him, calling him softly.

"Walter, darling, can you hear me?" she asked.

Walter made a small wave with his hand but did not answer. Mary knew that he had suffered serious injuries during his rescue and that it could take some time before he made a full recovery. She called the doctor on duty.

Dr. Williams entered the hospital room and greeted Mary. He walked over to Walter's bed and carefully observed his patient's vital signs.

"Good morning, Mrs. Jones. How is Walter today?" He asked.

Mary was part of his observations about her son's small gestures, and the doctor immediately noted them.

"I'm going to do a closer look to see if Walter has a reaction," he says. "If all goes well, this could be an encouraging sign."

Dr. Williams began to examine Walter, checking his reflexes and state of consciousness. Suddenly, he notices a change in Walter's encephalogram.

"Look here", he said to Mary, pointing at the screen. "The encephalogram produces a reaction."

Mary didn't immediately understand what this meant, but she knew it was good news. "What does that mean?" she asked.

"Simply put, it means that his brain responds to stimuli," says the doctor. "This is a positive sign, but we must remain cautious and continue to monitor his condition."

Mary smiled gratefully. "Thank you, Doctor. I hope he will wake up completely soon."

"We all want the same thing, Mrs. Jones," Dr. Williams says with a smile. "We will monitor him closely and do everything we can to help him recover as soon as possible."

Mary thanked the doctor and turned to her son again. She hoped that Walter would recover soon, and that they could all celebrate his recovery together.

After several hours of monitoring, signs of improvement in Walter's health were increasingly visible. He began to move his arms and legs slightly, and he finally opened his eyes. Mary and John rushed to him, their eyes filled with tears of joy and hope.

"Walter, darling, you're finally awake," Mary said, kissing him on the forehead.

Dr. Williams was immediately notified and rushed into the room. After examining Walter, he asked him a few questions to test his state of consciousness.

"Do you know where you are?" he asks softly.

Walter blinked, tempted to concentrate. "I… I don't really know anymore. I just remember a fight at school, and after everything is a blur."

Dr. Williams explained to him while he was in Slidewater Hospital that he had been in a coma for twenty five days, and that he had suffered a head injury during the fight at school.

Walter looks around, confused and worried. "How come I've been in a coma for so long? Am I going to be, okay?"

Mary and John took their son's hand, trying to reassure him as much as possible. "You're going to be fine, darling, we're here with you," Mary said with a smile.

Dr. Williams explained that Walter had suffered a significant head injury and that he was going to need a lot of rest and care to fully recover. He also needs to explain that Walter was going to have rehabilitation to regain his physical and cognitive abilities.

Walter seemed worried and frightened, but Mary and John stayed by his side to reassure and support him in his recovery. "We are here for you, my son. We will support you throughout your recovery," John says with a smile.

Walter smiled faintly at them, grateful to have a loving family by his side. He knew he was going to need time to recover, but he was relieved to know he had people to rely on during this difficult time.

Little by little, Walter begins to recover from his twenty-five-day coma. Doctors and nurses help him recover his physical and cognitive abilities, and he is progressing every day. Mary and John are still by his side, supporting him in his recovery, while his friends and acquaintances from high school visit him regularly.

One day, as one of his friends was coming out of his room, Walter heard this friend talking with a young boy in the hallway. Walter heard Bryan's first name. Walter was surprised to hear the name of Bryan, a boy he didn't know. He turned to his parents, who were sitting next to him, and asked them who Bryan was. Mary and John exchanged a puzzled look before John replied, "We don't know him, honey. But he's come to see you every day since you've been here in the hospital."

Walter was shocked and intrigued. Why did a boy he didn't know come to visit him every day? He began to think, tried to remember if he had ever heard of this Bryan before his coma, but nothing had occurred to him.

"I don't understand," Walter said, shaking his head. "I've never heard of this Bryan."

Mary placed a comforting hand on her son's shoulder. "Don't worry, honey. We try to find out who he is and why he comes to see you every day. For now, you need to focus on your recovery."

Walter nodded, but the plot haunted him. Why did a boy he didn't know come to visit him every day? He was eager to find out who Bryan was and why he was so imbued to his healing.

The following days, Walter had a lot of questions about this named Bryan and tried to remember everything he could about him. He asked his friends if they knew anyone named

Bryan, but no one seemed to know more than he did. He was frustrated that he couldn't remember this mysterious boy and he couldn't wait to get to know him to find out who he was.

Finally, after several days of waiting, Bryan enters Walter's room, smiling shyly. Walter turns to him, filled with conflicting emotions. He was happy to finally meet this boy who had given him so much support, but he was also confused and intrigued as to why Bryan cared so much about him.

Bryan is a seventeen-year-old with a thin, angular face. His dark brown hair is styled in a mess, giving the impression that he has just stood up. He has bangs that fall slightly on his forehead. His eyes are dark brown in color, with a bright and intelligent expression.

Bryan has a medium height and a slim, but athletic figure, suggesting that he is quite physically active. He has slightly tanned skin, perhaps due to a lot of time spent outdoors. He often wears casual clothes, such as jeans and t-shirts.

Upon closer inspection, Bryan notices that Bryan has light scars on his forehead and chin, indicating that he may have had minor accidents in the past. He also has a small dimple on his right cheek that becomes more pronounced when he smiles.

Overall, Bryan has an air of both confidence and sympathetic. His personality is probably as interesting as his appearance, with a keen intelligence and energy that attracts the attention of those around him.

"Hi, I'm Bryan!" the boy said with a warm smile.

Walter greeted him in turn, trying to contain his excitement and curiosity. "Thank you for coming to see me every day, Bryan. I really appreciate your support."

Bryan smiled again. "Of course, Walter. We don't quite know, but I know that you are a good person and that you deserve to be surrounded by support and affection."

Walter was touched by Bryan's words, but he was still intrigued by their relationship. "How did we meet?" he asked.

Bryan took a deep breath before replying, "Well, actually, we never really met before you were a coma. But I heard about you in a distant place, and I felt I needed to help you."

Bryan explains to Walter that he got to know his story through a mutual acquaintance and was touched by how Walter was a good friend and kind person. He came to visit her every day at the hospital, hoping to support him in his recovery and offer him a friendship. Walter was moved by Bryan's devotion and began to form a friendship with him.

As the days passed, Bryan and Walter grew closer and began to spend more time together. Bryan told Walter his own story and the two boys discovered that they had several interests in common. Bryan was passionate about music and played guitar, which interested Walter a lot.

The days continued to pass, and Walter improved at a steady pace. He began to walk more and more, to regain his strength and cognitive abilities. Mary and John were thrilled to see their son resume his normal life.

One day, Walter was visited by his doctor, who explained that his recovery had been quick and remarkable. He also added that it was time for Walter to begin his physical rehabilitation at home. Mary and John were thrilled to learn that their son would soon be coming home.

Before leaving, Walter warmly thanked Bryan for his friendship and support. They promised to stay in touch and see each other regularly. Walter also expressed his wish to meet Bryan with the person who told him Bryan about him, but Bryan explained that this person asked to remain anonymous.

12 – AFTER.

Walter was finally back home after a long convalescence in the hospital. He was happy to be back with his home and family, but something had been on his mind for several days. He wanted to know who had told Bryan about him. He had asked Bryan several times, but Bryan had always refused to give him the person's name.

One morning, when Bryan came to visit him, Walter decided to ask the question again. "Bryan, I can't help but think of that person who talked about me. Why don't you want to tell me his name?" He asks.

Bryan looks at Walter hesitantly. "You know, Walter, this person asked to remain anonymous. I don't want to betray his trust."

Walter frowned. "But why is it so important for me to know who it is?"

Bryan took a deep breath before replying, "Well, what I can tell you is that you have greetings from Alice, Mathilda and Jake."

Walter was shocked. These names were familiar to him, but he could not associate them with faces. "What do you mean by that?" he asks.

Bryan explained that these names were those of his former childhood friends. Friends he hadn't seen in years. "I'm sure you remember them, Walter. They have often been with you not long ago."

Walter tried to remember, but his memory was still fuzzy after his coma. He felt a mixture of emotions: sadness, anxiety, and hope. He wanted to see his friends again, but he didn't know where to find them.

"Bryan, could you find them for me? I want to see them again," he asked.

Bryan smiled. "Of course, Walter. I would do everything I could to find them."

Walter felt grateful to his friend and hoped that Bryan could find his friends. He couldn't wait to see them again and regain the memories he had lost.

Walter was thrilled that Bryan had agreed to help him find his friends, but he felt frustrated that he didn't remember them. He asked Bryan to help him identify them, give him details or anecdotes to help him remember their faces.

Bryan thought for a while before responding, 'Walter, I don't think I could help you in that way. You have to try to remember for yourself. Sometimes memories can be buried in our subconscious. You might try to remember something that is related to them."

Walter thought for a moment before nodding in agreement. He began to think about his childhood, trying to remember all the people he had met at that time. Soon after, he began to remember a strange world he had created in his mind.

"Bryan, I remember this strange world now. Alice, Mathilda, and Jake were my imaginary friends! Walter exclaims.

Bryan looks at him in surprise. "Really?"

Walter smiled. "Yes, I remember now. I invented a fantasy world where there were only children. There were no adults. I have experienced extraordinary things in this imaginary world."

Bryan looked Walter in the eye, walked up to him and said in a low voice. "Can you explain to me if his three people, Alice, Mathilda and Jake are imaginary people, how did they tell me to give you, their greetings?"

Walter felt baffled by Bryan's question. He had always believed that the fantasy world he had created was a figment of his imagination, but the mention of these familiar names had made him doubtful. He turns to Bryan and asks, "I don't know. Maybe this world I invented wasn't just in my head. Maybe these people were real."

Bryan tries to reassure Walter. "Don't worry, Walter. You've just come out of a long coma, it's normal for you to feel a little lost. But I'm sure these people were just characters you created in your fantasy world. Maybe you talked about them in your dreams or in your confusion after the coma."

Walter nodded, trying to understand what had happened. He had so many questions, but he didn't know how to phrase them. Finally, he asked, "But if it was just in my head, how could I have forgotten the information about them?"

Bryan thought before answering. "I think that's part of the side effects of a coma. You may have forgotten important things in your life, including those imaginary friends. But don't worry, you'll remember everything over time."

Walter felt a mixture of emotions in him. On the one hand, he was relieved that these people had not been real and that his memory had not betrayed her. On the other hand, he felt sad to know that this fantasy world he had created did not exist.

He began to reflect on this period of his life, trying to remember more details. Gradually, he remembered some memories that seemed to be related to his imaginary friends. He turns to Bryan with a smile on his face. "I now remember a few anecdotes about Alice, Mathilda, and Jake. I can't wait to see them again and tell them all about it."

Bryan smiled back. "I'm glad to hear you say that, Walter. I will do everything I can to find them, I promise you."

Walter remains puzzled by Bryan's comments. He wasn't sure how to find imaginary friends in a world that existed only in his mind. He asks Bryan, "How can you find Alice, Mathilda and Jake if this fantasy world was just a figment of my imagination?"

Bryan simply replies, "Because I know where they are."

Walter is even more puzzled. How could he know where imaginary characters were? He asks Bryan, "How do you know about the existence of this imaginary world?"

Bryan replies, "That's where I'm from."

Walter is astonished. He couldn't believe Bryan came from a world he had invented in his head. It was too incredible to be true. He had so many questions to ask, but he didn't know how to phrase them.

Bryan seemed to understand how Walter felt. He explains: "I know this is all difficult to understand, Walter, but you have to trust me. I'll explain everything you need to know, but you have to keep an open mind."

Walter nodded, trying to stay calm despite the excitement and confusion that overwhelmed him. "Okay, I'll do my best."

Bryan continued, "Remember that fantasy world you created, where there were only children and no adults? Well, it actually exists, but not in the sense that you understand it. It is a parallel world, an alternate reality where children can live without being confronted with the difficulties and responsibilities of adult life."

Walter was amazed. He couldn't believe his fantasy world was real. He asks Bryan, "How did you discover this world? And how can you access it?"

Bryan smiled. "I am an explorer of parallel worlds. I discovered this world a few years ago and have returned several times since. I even met Alice, Mathilda, and Jake."

Walter was even more astonished. He asked Bryan, "What are they like? Are they really as I imagined them?"

Bryan replied, "They are exactly as you imagined them. And they are looking forward to you, Walter. They have so much to tell you."

Walter was moved. He couldn't believe that he would finally meet his imaginary friends in real life. He turned to Bryan gratefully and said, "I trust you, Bryan. I am ready to follow you in this fantasy world."

Bryan smiled at Walter and said, “I know you just came out of a long coma, Walter, so I’ll explain everything to you in detail. You won’t even have to travel to get to this fantasy world. All you have to do is close your eyes and focus on your imaginary world. You have to remember every detail of your world, the colors, smells, sounds, the way children talk and behave. If you concentrate hard enough, you will find yourself in this parallel world. It’s very simple, but you have to be willing to believe it.”

Walter listened attentively to Bryan’s explanations, fascinated by what he heard. He clearly remembered his fantasy world and all the details he had created. He was so eager to go back and meet his imaginary friends.

But suddenly, a thought struck him: “How did you know I was looking for information about you in this parallel world?” he said to Bryan, a little nervous.

Bryan smiled and replied, "Jake told me that a young boy was learning about me in this world. Jake is a loyal friend and he wanted to make sure you were a trusted person before giving you more information about this fantasy world."

Walter was relieved. He feared that Bryan was not a trusted friend, but Jake's words reassured him. He now remembered that Jake was one of his closest imaginary friends.

"Walter are you ready to try?" asked Bryan, holding out his hand.

Walter took Bryan's hand, still a little uncertain. But he remembered Bryan's words: he had to believe for it to work. So he closed his eyes and focused on his imaginary world. He remembered every detail and every emotion he had created.

When he opened his eyes again, he was in a wonderful world, filled with color, joy and children's laughter. He was amazed by the beauty of this fantasy world. He then saw Alice, Mathilda and Jake running up to him with smiles on their faces. They kissed him and told him they were thrilled to finally see him again.

Walter was filled with joy and gratitude to Bryan. He couldn't believe that he had been able to return to his fantasy world and meet his friends. He finally felt free to be a child, without worries or responsibilities.

Bryan joined Walter, Mathilda, Alice, and Jake, who welcomed him warmly. Alice gave Bryan a big smile and thanked him for bringing Walter back to them. Bryan replied simply, "I promised you, didn't I?"

Jake then explained to Walter what had happened since he left the world of children. He told her that Alice had become the new president of the Grand Council of Children, after Yann was banished for wanting to take power by force. Walter was surprised, but happy for Alice, who had always been one of his favorite friends.

Mathilda was extremely moved to see Walter again. She began to cry with joy as she hugged him. Walter, thinking she was sad, asked her why she was crying. Mathilda then explained to him that it was not sadness, but happiness. She told him that the time of the children's world was not the same as in the real world, and that they had all been waiting so long to see him again.

Walter was touched by the affection of his friends. He felt like a child again, without worries or responsibilities. He asked them what they had done since he left, and they began to tell him all kinds of incredible adventures. Walter was fascinated by their stories and laughed out loud.

Bryan was smiling, happy to see Walter finally reunited with his friends. He told them that he had to leave, but that he would come back to see them soon. Walter thanked him with all his heart for allowing him to return to his fantasy world.

Before Bryan left, Walter timidly asked him how he could get home without his parents worrying. Bryan simply replied that he had to do the same technique as when he came into the world of children. Walter nodded, but he looked a little nervous about returning to the real world.

Walter's other friends noticed his concern and Jake asked him if he was afraid to return home. Walter nodded and confessed that he was apprehensive that everything he had experienced in the children's world was just a dream and that he would never be able to go back to it.

Mathilda gently put her hand on Walter's shoulder and said with an encouraging smile, "But you know it wasn't a dream, Walter. You were there, with us, all this time. And now that you're back, you can come back whenever you want!"

Walter smiled shyly, a little reassured by Mathilda's words. He was still a little dizzy after his long coma, but he felt happy to be surrounded by his friends. He had always loved their imaginary world, where anything was possible and where he could be himself without being judged.

He spent the next few days exploring the world of children with his friends, rediscovering familiar places, and exploring new places. He felt like a child again, amazed by everything around him. He often laughed and felt free from any worries.

Meanwhile, his parents were worried about his absence and searched everywhere for him. They had informed the police and distributed posters around the city, but no one seemed to know where he was. They were exhausted and worried, wondering if they would ever see their beloved son again.

Despite all this, Walter was happy to spend time with his friends in their fantasy world. He felt like he was regaining a part of himself that he had lost growing up. He felt free and happy, and he knew that his friends would always be there for him, no matter what happened.

After spending a few wonderful days with his friends in the children's fantasy world, Walter determined it was time to go home. He wanted to find his parents and tell them he was safe, but he also knew he would be back soon to see his friends again.

Before leaving, he said goodbye to Alice, Mathilda, and Jake. He promised them that he would come back soon, and that he was looking forward to discovering even more of this wonderful world. His friends gave him warm hugs and told him they were looking forward to him.

Walter arrived home just before dinner. His parents were shocked and happy to finally see him again. They had looked for him everywhere and feared the worst. Walter then explained to them what had happened. He tells them about his journey to the Imaginary Kingdom of Children and his wonderful friends.

"I met Alice, she is the new president of the Children's Grand Council," Walter tells his parents. "And I found Mathilda and Jake, my friends. They told me all kinds of amazing stories, and I even saw dragons and unicorns!"

His parents listened attentively, fascinated by their son's story. They couldn't believe it was all real. But they could see how happy and alive Walter was.

"I know it sounds crazy," Walter continued. "But it's real. I feel like a child again, without worries or responsibilities. I'm happy to be back, but I know I'll be back there soon. My friends are waiting for me."

Walter's parents smiled and hugged him. They were happy that their son was back, but they could also see how important this trip had been to him. They knew Walter had discovered something special, something that would change his life forever.

After returning home, Walter decided to resume his normal life and return to Slidewater City High School. He had friends there, but he kept his story and the encounter with the imaginary Kingdom of Children to himself. He didn't want people to think he was crazy or to be the laughingstock of school. He knew his experience was something special, but he preferred to keep it to himself.

Days passed and Walter struggled to resume his normal life. However, he often had blues strokes and felt lonely and isolated. He knew that his friends from the Imaginary Kingdom of Children were there for him, so he decided to visit Alice, Mathilda, and Jake from time to time. Whenever he was sad, he would leave for the imaginary Kingdom of Children and smile again.

He often went to the Enchanted Forest where he had first met Mathilda. They had long conversations about life and dreams, and Walter loved listening to Mathilda's wise advice. She had become something of a mentor to him, and he felt lucky to have such a wise and caring friend.

Alice, meanwhile, was always running from one end of the Kingdom to the other, making sure everything was in order. She was the kind of friend you could always count on, and Walter was glad he had found her. He enjoyed spending time with her and helping her with her daily tasks.

Jake was busy leading the Directorate of Homeland Security, but he always made sure he had time to spend with Walter. They loved to talk about their past adventures and dreams for the future. Jake was a loyal and loyal friend, and Walter felt lucky to have him as a friend.

One day, while Walter was walking through the imaginary Kingdom of Children, he saw a familiar face. It was Bryan, his friend with whom he shared their strange life experience. Bryan had also discovered the Imaginary Kingdom of Children, and they decided to visit Alice, Mathilda, and Jake together.

Over time, Walter has learned to live with his unique experience. He was always a little sad when he had to leave his friends in the Imaginary Kingdom of Children, but he was happy to return to his normal life. He knew that no matter what happened, he had fantastic friends to talk to and share his incredible adventures with. And he knew he could always return to the imaginary realm of children to find Alice, Mathilda, Jake, and Bryan.

ABOUT THE AUTHOR

Roger-Pierre LE GRASSE is a French author, born in June 1981 in Orléans, Loiret. Passionate about history and writing since childhood, he has written and published several collections of history and manuals under various pseudonyms. His love for fiction is evident in his engaging storytelling and imaginary worlds.

Roger-Pierre LE GRASSE's passion for the audiovisual field is also worth highlighting. He admires the works of acclaimed director Kenneth Johnson, who created iconic universes such as "V," "Alien Nation" and "Call Me Jimmy 5."

His unique blend of stories, fiction, and passion for visual media shines through in his writing. His published works showcase his talent and creativity.

Roger-Pierre LE GRASSE's work reflects his writing skills, his vast knowledge, and his overflowing imagination. Her love for the story, combined with her passion for storytelling, creates a unique reading experience that transports the reader to a different time and place.

www.ingramcontent.com/pod-product-compliance
Lightning Source LLC
La Vergne TN
LVHW012044160826
845678LV00014B/2700

* 9 7 8 2 4 9 3 1 4 6 0 9 0 *